NIKKI POWERGLOVES

And the Power Giver

David Estes

D1417192

Jacket art and design by Winkipop Designs

For all the INCREDIBLY creative kids in
Maine's Brewer Community School 3rd grade class of 2015.
You are awesome!

And for their teacher, Cherrie MacInnes, who goes well above
and beyond to give her students the best possible learning experience.
Thanks for everything!

Adventures

1

Power Island! Power Island! Power Island!

Nikki Powergloves couldn't stop smiling. Standing on top of Phantom's Peak with the wind in her hair, she had never felt better. Every time she thought about George Powerglasses's promise to guide her and her friends to the Power Island to find the Power Giver, her lips would automatically curl up on each side.

"What are you grinning about, Clown-Face?" Spencer asked. He opened the secret portal that led into the mountain.

"Your mom," Nikki said, still grinning. Nikki had recently discovered how funny "Your Mom" jokes could be. George Powerglasses knew about a thousand of them.

"Ha ha, very funny," Spencer said. "That was so funny I could only laugh on the inside."

"I was just thinking about—" Nikki started to say.

"The Power Island," Spencer finished. "I can read your mind like a book."

Nikki groaned. She could never keep secrets from her best friend. Spencer was a genius in a lot of ways, including mind reading, and he didn't even need superpowers to do it.

"Helloooooooo!" Spencer shouted into the tunnel. His voice echoed into the distance: HELLOOOOO! Helloooooo! Hellooooooooo! He turned back to her. "Are you ready to face the Power Giver?"

Nikki shrugged. She wasn't really sure. Over the last two days she'd gone home to see her parents and her dog, Mr. Miyagi. She'd eaten her mom's delicious home-cooked meals, lasagna and roast chicken and stir fry. Before Nikki left to return to the Power City, she hugged her mom and dad harder than she'd ever hugged them.

"What was that for?" her dad had asked, raising an eyebrow.

"Just...just because I love you guys," Nikki had said.

Now she wondered whether she would ever see her parents again. She hoped so, otherwise she would miss them too much.

"Nikki?" Spencer said, waving a hand in front of her face. "Earth to Nikki!"

"Oh...sorry!" Nikki said. "I was just thinking about—"

"Your parents," Spencer finished, once more reading her mind. Above them, the wind howled and the clouds swirled. Each cloud was a different color, like a beautiful rainbow.

Looking back at Spencer, Nikki nodded. "Do you think we'll ever see our parents again?"

"Of course!" Spencer exclaimed. "You're Nikki Powergloves and you've got a genius sidekick. We'll *always* come out on top."

Nikki wasn't so sure, but she appreciated her friend's optimism. She squeezed his hand. "Let's go. The other kids are waiting."

"Me first!" Spencer shouted, diving headfirst into the dark tunnel. He screamed a high-pitched scream and disappeared from sight.

Nikki laughed. Even though she was worried about missing her parents, she was so excited that it felt like a thousand tiny feathers were tickling the inside of her stomach. After all, today was THE DAY. George had asked all the members of the Power Team to return to the

Power City on this particular day, so they could leave for the Power Island together.

Nikki took a deep breath and then jumped into the hole. Soon she was screaming too, sliding down the biggest, twistiest, fastest slide in the whole world. Bright gold, blue, and red lights flashed on and off, illuminating funny pictures. Like a monkey giving a baby a piggyback ride. And a rhinoceros sprouting wings and flying high in the clouds. She giggled and giggled until the slide dropped suddenly, making her stomach fly up into her throat. And then she was free falling, emerging from the dark tunnel into a brightly lit cavern.

When she landed on the net next to Spencer, she bounced three times before coming to a stop. "Awesome," she breathed.

"Fun every time," Spencer agreed. "Do we have time to do it again?"

As much as Nikki wanted to say "yes," they had more important things to do today. "Sorry, Spence, but we're already late."

A giant metal claw was already moving overhead, eventually stopping directly above them. With a lurch, the claw dropped down and picked them up. "Whee!" Spencer yelled, rocking the claw back and forth as it transported them over the net and onto the ground.

Once they were on their feet, they wasted no time. They ran through a large arched doorway, past a bunch of robots and vehicles moving around on their own, and down the first tunnel on the right. This particular tunnel was called the banana tunnel, and as they ran, an enormous yellow banana unpeeled itself on each side. "Smells like a good day," Spencer said, sniffing the air.

The next tunnel was called the wormhole, because hundreds of wriggly, slimy earthworms slid through the dirt walls and ceiling. There were even some worms squirming under Nikki's feet, and she had to do a funny dance to avoid stepping on them. "Ew," she said. "I hate this tunnel." Normally she would avoid going this way, but it was the fastest route to Weebleville, bypassing the purple couch room.

Weebleville was the meeting place for today, and she didn't want to be late.

Spencer grabbed a worm and tried to stick it in Nikki's face, but she used the power of the orange glove she was wearing to race away from him at super speed. "No fair, Speedy-Gonzalez!" Spencer said, running after her.

They passed through three more tunnels—one made of soft cotton, one made of bouncy rubber, and one made of chocolate candy bars—and then stepped into the last tunnel before Weebleville, the fire tunnel. As Nikki marched between the torches hanging on each side of the tunnel, she licked chocolate off of her fingers. Spencer did the same. Anytime they passed through the chocolate bar tunnel they always ran their fingers along the walls to get them nice and chocolaty. "Mmm," they said together.

After a few minutes, the end of the tunnel came into view, a big stone door blocking their way. WEEBLEVILLE was written in shaky handwriting above the door. Loud voices were rumbling behind the stone, but Nikki couldn't understand what they were saying until she got closer.

Her eyes widened when she figured it out. The voices were chanting as one. "Power Island! Power Island! Power Island!"

Nikki and Spencer looked at each other, smiles forming on their lips. Together, they each grabbed a part of the door and heaved it open.

2

I am the greatest power kid

Naomi was tired of being angry all the time, but she couldn't seem to be happy anymore. She'd lost her biggest fight yet, all because of that annoying George Powerglasses guy. She'd also lost her entire gang of Power Outlaws when they joined Nikki's stupid Power Team.

"Stupid George," she muttered under her breath. "Stupid Power Team, stupid Power Giver." She looked at the skirt she was wearing, black with green polka dots. It gave her the ability to change her powers rapidly. Not that it mattered. It was pointless having powers when she wasn't even a part of the Power Rankings anymore. She was just an outcast now. "Stupid skirts."

Her sidekick, Slobber, wasn't really helping her mood. A few days ago he'd found a bucket of colored chalk. He'd been drawing pictures of the Power Team ever since. There was Nikki Powergloves and Freddy Powersocks and all the rest. He was even drawing their freaky little sidekicks. In fact, Slobber had just about finished his picture of the amateur magician, Chilly Weathers.

"Stupid sidekick," Naomi muttered.

"What wash that, bossh?" Slobber asked.

"Did I say you could speak?" Naomi said sharply, putting her hands on her hips.

"No, but—" A line of drool ran from Slobber's mouth to his drawings on the cement.

"Did I say you could drool?" Naomi asked.

"No, but—"

"Did I say you could do *anything*?"

Slobber closed his mouth, although spit continued to run down his chin.

"That's better," Naomi said. "You're MY sidekick. You jump when I say you can jump, you draw when I say you can draw, and you drool when I say you can drool."

Slobber drooled.

"Stop that!"

Using his shirt, Slobber wiped away the drool and clamped his lips together tightly, trying to hold back the spittle. Naomi looked her sidekick up and down. His shoes were untied and his shorts and shirt coated with powdery chalk dust. "Hmm," Naomi said. Unlike her, he was far from perfect. From a young age, Naomi's parent's had expected perfection from her. Getting the top score on a test was only good enough if she got 100%. Missing a single answer meant she'd have to study twice as hard for the next test. Once, when she got second place in a school spelling bee, her father was so angry that he made her walk home. "Win next time," he said. "Or you can walk everywhere." She won the next spelling bee, and the one after that, and every single competition since. Whatever it took, she had to win at everything she did, or she would disappoint her parents. And that included winning the Power Rankings.

Slobber's face was turning red. Naomi realized he was holding his breath. "Breathe!" she yelled. "You don't need my permission to breathe, stupid!"

11

Slobber released his breath and sucked in more air, slobbering all over his own shoes in the process. Naomi shook her head. If her sidekick wasn't so freakishly big and strong, he'd be completely useless. Instead, he was all she had left.

"Why do you keep drawing the Power Team?" she asked.

He looked startled, his hands clutching each other nervously. "I, um, I just, well—"

Naomi tapped her toe. "I don't have all day!" She didn't know why she kept shouting, but she couldn't seem to stop. She was just so...so...*angry*.

Slobber wiped away more drool and said, "I just thought maybe we could eventually, you know, join the Power Team."

"No," Naomi said immediately.

"But they've invited us."

Naomi didn't need to be reminded. Twice in the last two days that pathetic George Poweglasses dude had slid down his rainbow and handed her a card. Then he'd created a beautiful white Pegasus and flown away without saying a word. Naomi didn't have the cards anymore, because she'd ripped them into a thousand pieces and fed them to her flock of attack pigeons. Each card had said the same thing:

Naomi Powerskirts and sidekick Slobber,
You are hereby invited to join the Power Team at your earliest convenience.
Please don't wait too long or we'll be forced to leave for the Power Island without you.
Meet us at Weebleville.
Sincerely,
George Powerglasses (on behalf of the Power Team)

Just thinking about their stupid message made Naomi cringe. Join them? Really? They were all a bunch of goobers who didn't know a great power from a freckle. But still...maybe her slobbering sidekick was on to something.

"You really want to join the Power Team, huh?" she asked.

Slobber nodded, drool spilling from his lips like a leaky faucet.

Naomi tapped her toe and cracked her knuckles, remembering how quickly Sue the Perfect Barbie Doll had joined the Power Team. Maybe Sue was just being sneaky. Maybe she was being smarter than Naomi. "Hmm," Naomi said. "Maybe you're right."

"I am?" Slobber said.

"Well, you said something smart, but I don't think you said it on purpose, so it's really *my* idea and not yours. Do you understand?"

Slobber just stared at her like a hideous reflection in the mirror. The anger rushed into Naomi like a crashing wave. Rapidly, she changed her skirt to her pink gymnastics one, did a double front flip with a twist, and landed on Slobber, knocking him hard to the ground. She stared down at him. "I said: Do. You. Understand?"

Eyes wider than traffic lights, he nodded.

"Good," Naomi said. "We'll leave immediately. We'll be joining the Power Team after all. But only so we can win. Only so we can destroy them all on the Power Island. Only so we can find the Power Giver and rise to the top of the Power Rankings."

"That doesn't sound very nice," Slobber said.

"I am the greatest power kid," Naomi said. "But not because I'm nice. Because I always win."

3

Butt-bouncin' good

"Power Island! Power Island! Power Island!" The chant got louder and louder as Nikki and Spencer walked through Weebleville. The streets were empty of both Weebles and kids, which was very unusual. Normally the Weebles would be dancing and playing. Instead, they'd left behind all their toys, inflatable beach balls and water guns and Nerf Frisbees and even rolls of white toilet paper.

"Power Island! Power Island! POWER ISLAND! POWER ISLAND!" As they got closer, the sound became deafening.

Nikki and Spencer dodged the debris, making their way to a big square in front of the tall tower where the Great Weeble lived. That's where they discovered the source of the noise.

"POWER ISLAND! POWER ISLAND!" chanted the Weebles and kids.

"Hey, Nikki! Spencer!" someone shouted. Nikki spotted Samantha in the crowd, pushing and shoving her way past the prickly porcupine-beavers to get to her.

"Hey, Sam," Nikki said. "Are we on time?"

Samantha smiled. "Yes, we're still waiting on a couple of power kids." It was hard to hear her friend's voice over the sound of the Weebles' chanting.

Amidst the cacophony, other members of the Power Team were crowding around them now too, Freddy and Mike and Britney and Tanya. Their sidekicks, Chilly and Dexter, were also there. Tyrone and his sidekick, Weasel, stood nearby. Weasel was balanced on Tyrone's shoulders and smirking at Nikki. Peter Powerhats was sitting behind the wheel of a giant monster truck, revving the engine. Sue and her sidekick, Sharkey, were pretending not to notice Nikki's arrival, but Nikki could tell they were watching very carefully. Even though Sue had joined the Power Team, Nikki still didn't really trust her. All she seemed to care about was herself and winning whatever prize the Power Giver was planning to give the winner of the Power Rankings.

Nikki considered who was still missing. "Where are Jimmy and Axel?" she asked.

Samantha shrugged. "No-shows so far."

Nikki really hoped Jimmy would come, but she knew he was still struggling with whether it was okay to use his powers. He had really changed since the first time she met him, when all he wanted to do was destroy things. Now he seemed to only want to help. "Tanya," Nikki said. "You've been talking to Jimmy a lot, right?"

Tanya ducked her head a little, as if surprised Nikki had asked her a question. "Well, yeah, I guess so." Her face was turning fire-engine red at all the attention.

"Do you think he'll come?" Nikki asked, smiling and nodding. Tanya sometimes needed to be encouraged to speak.

Tanya managed a small smile of her own and lifted her chin. "Yes. Yes, I think he'll come."

"Good. What about Axel?" Nikki asked. "Has anyone spoken to him and Juniper?"

Everyone shook their heads. Nikki's heart sank. Without Axel and his awesome sidekick, June the Goon, facing the Power Island would be far more difficult.

"They'll come too," Spencer said, patting her on the back. "I know it." Spencer's confidence made Nikki feel a little better. Her sidekick's predictions were almost always right.

"What about Naomi?" Tyrone asked, his strong voice carrying above the ruckus.

"What about her?" Sue said, finally coming closer.

"George said he invited her too," Tyrone said. "He said we'd have a better chance on the Power Island if Naomi joined the Power Team."

"Blech," Sue said. "We don't need her. Trust me, I know Naomi, and she's like a thorn stuck in your thumb that you can never get out."

For once, Nikki agreed with Sue. Naomi had never done anything but try to hurt her and her friends. Nikki really hoped Naomi stayed away from Weebleville until they were long gone and headed for the Power Island.

That's when Jimmy showed up. Well, more like walked right through one of the walls of the Great Weeble's tower. He was like a ghost, walking through the crowd, stepping right through the Weebles instead of going around them. Some of them giggled and bobbed up and down on their rear ends. "Jimmy's butt-bouncin' good!" one of them said.

Nikki didn't know what that meant, but seeing Jimmy made her smile. "Glad you could make it," she said, extending her hand for a high five.

Jimmy looked at her hand for a moment, chewing his lip, and then slapped it. "Thank you," he said. "I hope I can help the team."

"You will," Nikki said. "I know it."

Before Jimmy could respond, George Powerglasses appeared overhead, riding his snow-white Pegasus. As he soared over them, a cheer went up from the Weebles and kids, and then slowly died down, until there was complete silence. The Pegasus landed in the middle of the square, folding its purple wings at its sides. George's Google Glasses matched his flying horse's wings perfectly. Everyone waited for him to speak. Everyone except Sue.

"Is it *finally* time to go?" Sue asked. "Waiting to go to the Power Island is more boring than watching Spencer sort through his superhero underwear collection."

Nikki glared at Sue. She didn't care if Sue made fun of her, but it was not okay to make fun of her sidekick. The only problem was that Spencer *did* like to sort through his superhero underwear collection and it *was* really boring.

Sue ignored Nikki and stared at George, waiting for his response.

George tipped his purple glasses down on his nose and looked out over the crowd. "I don't see Axel," he said.

"Who cares," Sue said. "We don't need him."

"Yes, we do," Nikki said, stepping forward.

"No, we don't," Sue said, moving closer to Nikki. Nikki had the urge to use her super-speed to run up to Sue and tackle her. She took a deep breath. *No,* she told herself. *We're supposed to be a team.*

Nikki didn't know what else to say, but thankfully George did. "Nikki's right," George said. "Without Axel, we're not leaving."

"Grrr," Sue growled in frustration. "I can't take another minute in this...this...*place*! These *creatures* are disgusting! Look at them!" All around Sue, the Weebles were bouncing on their butts, grinning big, toothy grins.

Nikki knew Naomi meant the Weebles, but she didn't think of them as creatures, and they certainly weren't disgusting. Mildly rude and sometimes irritating, yeah, but mostly funny and weird. She considered the Weebles to be her friends.

Luckily, Axel showed up just when it looked like Sue might start using the Weebles as kick balls. He was in slinky form, rattling toward them in long slinky strides. Dark-haired Juniper was riding Axel the Slinky, leaping from prong to prong with each step. She looked awesome.

"Finally!" Sue said.

Axel transformed back into himself. He was wearing a heavy gray wool jacket with a picture of a slinky on it. He was also wearing a mischievous grin as he looked at his watch. "Right on time," he said in a strong English accent.

"Sorry," June said, apologizing for her superhero. "He insisted on waiting until the last possible minute. I've been trying to get him to come for hours."

Nikki didn't care about any of that. She was just glad Axel was here. Now the entire Power Team was in one place at one time. Surely that meant they could leave for the Power Island.

"You're still missing one power kid," George said.

Nikki frowned. "What? No, everyone's here." She looked around, trying to see if she'd forgotten anyone. *Nope.*

"Naomi," George said.

"But you said we could go without her," Sue complained.

"I lied," George said. "The Power Giver won't let any of you on the Power Island unless *all* of you go. You have to be a team."

Sue blew out an exasperated breath. "This is a waste of time. Naomi will never show." Sharkey clacked her teeth together in agreement.

"She might," George said.

Sue balled her fists and looked ready to face George *and* his Pegasus. "If you think Naomi is going to show her face around here, you're even dumber than you loo—"

There was a flash of light and Naomi appeared, with Slobber standing at her side, blinking away spots from his eyes.

"Hey losers," Naomi said, winking right at Nikki. "Did you miss me?"

4

Fake tears

Sue felt like throwing up all over her slippers. This was *not* the way things were supposed to go. Naomi was supposed to be the dumb villain who was too angry to make smart decisions. And yet here she was. Ready to join the Power Team.

"I vote against her," Sue said, flashing the biggest, fakest, most white-teethed smile she could muster. It was something she'd learned while on the beauty pageant circuit. "They'll never know you don't mean it," her mother had taught her. Her mother was once Miss Georgia, so she would know.

"Are we really going to vote?" Nikki asked. *Grrr.* Sue was so sick and tired of Nikki Powergloves. She wasn't even *pretty*. Well, not really. Sure, she was sort of cute in a boring country girl kind of way. But she wasn't beautiful the way Sue was. Sue had won every beauty pageant in her county since the age of three! Yeah, maybe she hated getting all dressed up and primped, preened, and painted, but still. She won every time. "You're a winner, just like me," her mother had told her time and time again.

Everyone looked to George for a decision. As much as Sue hated it, he seemed to be the one in charge. George's glasses changed from that horrid purple color to reflective silver and his flying horse disappeared. Sue remembered what those glasses could do. She remembered how Naomi had tried to hit George with a bolt of electricity and George reflected it back at her. Naomi's hair had stuck straight up! Sue had never laughed so hard in her life. But still, she didn't want George using his glasses on her.

George said, "Yes. The Power Team has to vote. You're a team now."

Something about the way George said it made Sue wonder about something. "What about you? Do you get a vote?"

George shook his head. "I'm just your guide to the Power Island. I can't make decisions for the Power Team."

Sue smiled. That was good. *Very* good. "Then as I said, I vote NO." Sue winked at Naomi, who just glared at her. Even when Naomi was angry, she was really pretty. Beautiful even. With long glossy black hair and dark intelligent eyes, Sue knew Naomi was her biggest competition. "Everyone else should vote NO too. Naomi is bad news. She tried to hurt all of you."

"So did you," Samantha said, stepping forward.

"Only because Naomi made me," Sue said, her voice honey sweet. It was a bold lie, but she knew if she said it nice enough, they would believe her.

"Liar!" Naomi screamed. She raised her fist as if to attack, but George was already stepping between them.

"I wouldn't do that," he said.

Naomi backed away, standing next to her slobbering sidekick. "I—I—I—" Naomi stuttered.

"You what?" Sue said. "You want to cry?"

Naomi's face changed from angry to sad in a moment. She was blinking furiously, as if, as if...Sue couldn't believe her eyes...Naomi was actually crying, tears dripping down her cheeks in hot waterfalls.

"I'm sorry!" Naomi cried. "I did a lot of bad stuff, and I'm sorry. I just want to be on the team."

Sue's mouth fell open. She knew *exactly* what Naomi was doing, because she'd done it a thousand times to fool a thousand people to get what she wanted. Fake tears. Naomi was using fake tears, pushing them out from her eyes. *Oh, you're good, girl*, Sue thought. *But not good enough to fool me.* "She doesn't mean it," Sue said, pointing a finger at Sue. "She's lying."

"She's crying," the silly curly-haired redhead said. Sue couldn't remember her name—Courtney or Whitney or something.

"Trust me, she's faking it," Sue said. "She's acting sad to get the rest of you to vote her onto the team."

"Why would you think that?" Nikki asked. "Because it's something *you* would do?"

Sue clamped her mouth shut. Nikki Powergloves was smarter than she thought. "Just vote," Sue growled.

"I vote yes," Nikki said. "I don't like Naomi any more than the rest of you, but George said we'll need her on the Power Island, and I believe him."

"Sorry, Nikki," Samantha said, "but I have to vote no. Naomi has done nothing but hurt us."

"It's okay," Nikki said. "I understand. How about the rest of you?"

Sue watched as each kid voted. Even the sidekicks got a vote. Sharkey chomped her teeth together and voted no. Sue tried to count up all the votes, but lost track. It was going to be close. When the last kid voted, George said, "There were eight votes against Naomi. And...*nine* votes for Naomi. Congratulations, Naomi Powerskirts, you and your sidekick are the last two members of the Power Team!"

Naomi smiled and her tears dried up. Slobber drooled happy drool. Some Weebles cheered, but most booed. Tyrone and Weasel went over to Naomi and Slobber and patted them on the back, welcoming them to the team.

And Sue ground her teeth so hard her jaw started to hurt.

Naomi had managed to fool enough of the kids to get on the team, just like Sue had. She knew only one of them could be champion, and it wasn't going to be Naomi.

5

The island is here, the island is there, the island is everywhere (and nowhere)

Nikki didn't want to spend any more time with Naomi than she had to, but she also knew that they'd never make it to the Power Island and get the chance to meet the Power Giver unless all of the power kids were on the team. Naomi hadn't fooled her with her fake tears or her false apology, but Nikki still had to vote for her.

"You better not try to hurt any of my friends," Nikki whispered to Naomi after the voting was over.

Naomi stuck her tongue out. "You better sleep with one eye open," she said.

Nikki wasn't planning to sleep at all if she could help it. At least not until after they'd found the Power Giver.

Weebleville grew quiet as a tiny black Weeble clambered onto George's shoulders. "QUIET Y'ALL!" the Great Weeble shouted, even though everyone was already quiet. "Listen up. George gots sum important infermayshun 'bout the Power Island."

Nikki inched forward. Just the thought of the Power Island made Nikki want to take off into the air and do figure eights.

With the Great Weeble still on his shoulders, George said, "The Power Island is nearly impossible to find."

"Why?" Spencer asked from beside her. Nikki sighed. *Why?* was Spencer's favorite question. He *always* had to know why something was the way it was. He told her that sometimes he couldn't sleep if there was a question he didn't know the answer to. *Intellectual curiosity* he liked to call it.

George reached in his pocket and pulled something out. A model of an island, split into two parts. One side was a huge black mountain. It looked like the mountain's peak had been chopped off, and there were red lines running down its sides. The other side was full of all different kinds of trees, like a jungle.

"This is a replica of the Power Island," George said. "Sometimes the island is here." With a quick thrust, he moved the model over to the side. "And sometimes the island is there. The Power Island is everywhere and nowhere, all at the same time."

"That doesn't make sense," Spencer said.

"Do kids being able to fly and burp fireballs and stop time make more sense?" George asked.

Spencer didn't have a response to that. In a funny way, Nikki actually enjoyed seeing her sidekick run out of words.

"The Power Island is always moving. Sometimes it's bobbing in the Pacific Ocean and sometimes it sinks deep under the sea."

"Like Atlantis?" Spencer said, finding his voice again.

"Sort of," George said. "But not an underwater city. An underwater island. And sometimes the Power Island flies above the world, hovering over places like France, China, or even South Dakota and Maine."

Nikki thought the idea of a moving island was pretty cool, but she was worried about one thing. "Won't we fall off when the island moves?"

George laughed. "Maybe," he said, which didn't exactly comfort Nikki at all. "But the most important thing is that you all work together."

"But aren't we competing?" Sue asked. "Aren't we all trying to knock Nikki off the top of the Power Rankings?" Sue smiled a dazzling smile when she said the part about Nikki. Nikki clenched her fists, wishing she could vote Sue off the team.

George said, "Yes and no. The Power Giver will rank you based on your performance on the island, but you have to be a team if you want to make it to the end. No fighting. Promise me."

Heads bobbed back and forth as the power kids and their sidekicks looked at each other. "We promise!" they said together. Nikki noticed the way Sue's fingers were crossed behind her back as she said it. She wondered how many other kids would break their promise once they were on the island.

"And remember, I'll be watching you the whole time," George said, his glasses morphing to neon pink. "Don't make me use my favorite power."

"What can you do with those glasses?" Spencer asked.

"Drive a monster truck," George said, and suddenly a monster truck appeared with George sitting behind the wheel.

"Hey!" Peter Powerhats said. "That's *my* power!" His blue hat had disappeared and was now sitting on George's head.

"And turn into a slinky," George said. The monster truck vanished and George was a slinky.

"What the heck?" Axel said. His jacket was gone.

George turned back into himself. He was wearing Axel's jacket. He said, "And run with super-speed." Nikki felt a rush of cold in her hands and her orange gloves evaporated into thin air. A moment later they appeared on George's hands. His body was a blur as he raced around the room with the speed that Nikki usually had.

When he reappeared, the gloves vanished from his hands. Nikki felt a powerful warmth in her hands and the gloves reappeared, covering her fingers.

"How—how did you do that?" she asked.

"Using these"—he tapped his pink glasses—"I can steal whatever powers you're wearing. If you don't fight each other, I won't have to steal your powers. But if you do…well…just don't, okay?"

Most of the kids nodded, including Nikki. She didn't want anyone stealing her powers.

"What about the power kids' birthdays?" Spencer asked.

"Oh, yes," George said. "Thanks for reminding me. How many days until you all turn ten years old?"

With each passing day, Nikki had been counting down to her birthday. "Two," she said. "Two days left."

"Right," George said. "In two days you'll all turn ten years old, at the exact same moment. You are all connected to each other because of when you were born. That's why you're here, that's why you were selected to receive powers. That's why you're on the Power Team. When you turn ten, if you haven't found the Power Giver and completed all of his challenges, your powers will disappear and be lost forever."

Nikki swallowed the spit stuck in her throat. Losing her powers was something she didn't want to think about. They *had to* find the Power Giver. They just had to.

"What about you?" Spencer asked.

"What about me?" George said.

"Don't you turn ten on the same day, at the same time? Why are you working for the Power Giver and not a part of the Power Team?" Spencer's eyebrows were knitted together as he puzzled over the many questions bouncing around in his brain.

George nodded. "Good question. I was also born on the same day as all the power kids, but I was born one second later than all of you. The Power Giver gave me my powers, but asked me to help him with the competition without competing. I said yes."

A question popped into Nikki's mind. "Do you have a powerchest? You always change your glasses so fast. How do you do that?"

George chuckled. "I don't have a powerchest. The Power Giver gave me one pair of glasses, and told me they could change into all kinds of different glasses with different powers."

"How many powers?" Spencer asked. Nikki grinned at her sidekick. The two of them were keeping George plenty busy with all their questions.

"Thirteen," George said.

"No fair!" Naomi said. "We only have twelve powers each. *And* you can steal our powers."

"Life isn't fair sometimes," George said. "Deal with it." That shut Naomi up, which made Nikki very happy. "Any other questions?"

Spencer opened his mouth to speak, but Sue said, "No more questions, boy nerd, or whatever your name is."

"It's Spencer Quick, boy genius," Spencer said.

"Whatever," Sue said. "By the time we get to the island, we'll have turned ten and all this will be pointless. Let's just go already."

But Spencer couldn't help himself, he just had to ask one final question. "Are the Weebles coming too?"

At that, a cheer went up from the mob of Weebles, who started doing flips and cartwheels. Nikki even saw one Weeble shoot another one out of a cannon. "I'll answer that partickular question," the Great Weeble said. "We're goin' HOME!!!"

The rest of the Weebles starting chanting "HOME! HOME! HOME!"

It all made sense to Nikki now. Where the Weebles came from and why no one had ever seen them before they started popping up to give powerchests to kids.

The Weebles were from the Power Island, where they lived with the Power Giver, and now they were finally going home.

6

Welcome to the Power Island. Try not to die!

Nikki felt kind of silly. The entire Power Team was standing in a circle, holding hands. George had told them where to stand, and was now in the middle of the circle, wearing his yellow sunburst glasses. Nikki got to hold Spencer's hand on one side. That was great. She was used to his hand, which was always a little bit sweaty and cold, but didn't bother her. But on the other side she was stuck holding Naomi's hand. The girl's hand was really hot, almost as if her blood was made of fire. And Naomi kept squeezing Nikki's hand harder and harder until it started to ache.

"Stop that," Nikki whispered.

"Stop what?" Naomi said, smirking.

Nikki wished she was wearing her purple super-strength glove. Then she would show Naomi just how hard *she* could squeeze.

In the middle of the ring, George began spinning in a circle, faster and faster, until he looked like a tornado. Just watching him was making Nikki dizzy.

When George stopped, there was a flash of bright yellow light, blinding her. She heard some of the other kids shouting and screaming. Britney shrieked and Slobber shouted, "What'sh happening?"

It was like the whole world had disappeared, replaced by only the blinding light of the sun. Nikki couldn't feel her arms, or her legs, or anything. She couldn't feel the ground either. She couldn't tell if she was floating or flying or still standing in the cavern in Weebleville.

She blinked and the world reappeared. She was no longer in the Power City, no longer in Weebleville. She was lying on something wet and gritty.

Blink, blink. The sun was in her eyes, so she raised a hand to block it. She heard a sound. It was sort of a soft swishing, over and over again. Something cold was tickling her toes so she looked down at her feet. A gentle bubbly wave washed over her legs. She was lying on a beach, pressed into the sand. A small blue crab skittered past, walking sideways. "Getta offa mya beacha!" the crab said in what Nikki thought sounded like an Italian accent.

Nikki didn't know what to say. She'd never talked to a crab before.

"Chill out, Cranky," a voice said from nearby. "They're with me. They're the Power Team." George's shadow settled over Nikki, blocking out the sun.

"I-yah don'ta care if they'ra the Kings and Queens of Sweden," the Cranky Crab said. "Getta them offa mya beacha!"

"Ignore him," George said, offering Nikki a hand. "He's not nice to anyone." As George helped Nikki to her feet, the crab scuttled away muttering something in Italian under his breath.

"Thanks," Nikki said, looking around. All of the other power kids and their sidekicks were pulling themselves to their feet, blinking and taking in their surroundings. It almost looked like they were survivors from a shipwreck, washed up onto a deserted island. The only thing missing was all the broken stuff from the wrecked ship. The sky was a sea of vibrant blue, broken up by islands of clouds. The clouds were strangely golden, as if the sun had infused its light within them. *Odd*, Nikki thought.

Nikki spotted Spencer racing down the beach. "Surf's up!" he yelled, and plunged into the clear, turquoise water. When he bobbed up, he was grinning. "Come on in, the water's warm!"

Nikki shrugged. She was already pretty soaked from lying in the wet sand, and the water looked really refreshing on such a hot day, so she charged in after Spencer. Soon they were splashing each other with water and having a good time. The rest of the Power Team followed, laughing and playing. Some of them even changed their powers before coming in the water. Samantha was wearing a blue belt and was able to breathe underwater like a fish. Jimmy used his water control powers to create a waterspout. It pushed him high into the air and he sat on it like a throne. George's glasses turned blue and he sprouted fins and flippers, transforming into a dolphin. The kids took turns hanging onto his fins and getting pulled through the water.

Only Naomi, Sue, and their sidekicks stayed on the beach, sitting as far away from each other as possible. "Party poopers!" Spencer yelled at them.

Sharkey snapped her teeth together and said, "Don't make me come in there and be a real shark!"

Eventually, however, George turned back into a boy and motioned for them all to come back onto the beach. Wet, but happy, the kids ran out of the surf and onto dry sand, gathering around the one power kid who knew the Power Giver and where to find him. Nikki wrung out her shirt as best she could. Under the hot island sun, she expected her clothes and hair to dry quickly.

"Listen up," George said. "I'll be watching everything you do on the Power Island. But it's not my job to be your guide. That's someone else's job."

"Who?" Spencer asked.

George grinned. "I think it's time you met the 14th and final power kid."

A rush of excitement filled Nikki's chest. *Another power kid?* She was shocked when George appeared for the first time, and now he was telling them there was one more? She squeezed her fists in anticipation.

But not everyone shared her excitement at George's announcement. Naomi stalked forward until she was nose to nose with George. "You never said anything about another power kid," she said, pressing her finger to George's chest.

Nikki was impressed when George didn't move an inch. "You never asked," he said.

Naomi leaned forward even more, until she was practically breathing on George. "Do we have to compete against the 14th power kid too?"

George took a step back. Nikki didn't think he looked scared, but maybe Naomi had bad breath or something. "No, of course not. Seth was born one second after the other twelve power kids, too, just like me. The Power Giver asked for his help with the Power Rankings, just like he asked me."

Apparently satisfied, Naomi returned to Slobber's side and crossed her arms.

Britney raised her hand in the air, looking kind of nervous. "Yes, Britney?" George said.

Britney looked at her feet. Her red curls dangled in wet knots around her face. "I, uh, well, so Seth is the 14th power kid?"

George opened his mouth to speak, but before he could say a word, Freddy pointed at the sky and shouted, "Look!" Something blue and white streaked through the air, heading their way.

"It's a bird!" Mike yelled.

"It's a plane!" Tyrone said.

The blue/white thing shouted, "No! It's UnderMan!"

"Not again," Nikki heard George mutter under his breath. And then: "Outta the way! Outta the way!"

The kids scattered to the sides. Nikki's feet felt like lead as she tried to run through the sand, which was as thick as quicksand. In her peripheral vision she saw something blue and white careening toward her.

"Incoming!" the blue/white thing screamed.

"Oomf," Nikki said as a scrawny kid slammed into her. His feet tangled with her feet, his arms with her arms. They tumbled chins over bootstraps across the beach until, eventually, they stopped.

Nikki shook her head to clear the cobwebs. "Blech!" she exclaimed, spitting sand from her mouth.

A boy with pasty white skin stood before her. *How had he gotten back on his feet so quickly?* she wondered to herself. He wore small circular glasses, a blue jumpsuit, and a big toothy smile. His hands were on his hips. And he was wearing something else. Something strange.

"Is that…is that *underwear?*" Nikki asked, pointing at the tight white underwear the boy was wearing on the outside, over his blue jumpsuit.

"Pretty snazzy, huh?" the boy said.

"Uh…" Nikki wasn't sure what to say. Wearing underpants on the outside was…unusual. It reminded her of the time Spencer wore his underwear on his head to try to distract the Power Outlaws.

The rest of the Power Team were heading their way. Spencer was the first to arrive. He extended his hand. "You must be Seth Powerundies," Spencer said. "I'm Spencer Quick, boy genius. I'm Nikki's sidekick."

"The world shall call me UnderMan!" Seth Powerundies declared, raising his hands in the air.

"Sure, no problem," Spencer said. "Nice to meet you, UnderMan." They shook hands.

The rest of the kids gathered around them. George tried to whisper something to Seth, but Nikki heard every word. "I told you not to use your slingshot anymore. It's too dangerous."

"Danger is my middle name," Seth said.

"Nice landing, pipsqueak," Naomi said. "Maybe you should go to superhero training school to learn how to use your powers."

It wasn't a very nice thing to say, but Seth kept on smiling as if Naomi had just complimented him. "I will take that under consideration," he said.

Although she felt embarrassed about it, Nikki couldn't stop looking at the white underpants Seth wore on the outside of his jumpsuit. There was a picture of a slingshot on them. "You shot yourself out of a slingshot?" she asked.

Seth's smile widened and he nodded. "Pretty cool, huh? You probably thought I was flying, but I was really just falling." He laughed into his hand. "I'm still working on the landing."

Even though the 14th power kid was so small and scrawny he looked like he was six years old, Nikki liked him. He was nice and kind of funny. She could even get past the fact that he was wearing his underwear on the outside of his clothes.

Apparently, others couldn't. "Why are you wearing your underwear on the outside?" Sue asked.

Seth's eyes widened when he turned and saw Sue. He stepped forward and took her hand. "I didn't know there was a beautiful princess amongst you," he said, kissing her hand.

"Yuck!" Sue said, pulling away and wiping her hand on her shirt.

Seth wasn't fazed by Sue's reaction to his kiss. "I will defend you to the end, my lady!" he declared boldly. Nikki thought he sounded like a knight defending a damsel in distress from a dragon. She giggled and looked at Spencer. Spencer was laughing too. She had a feeling Seth would get along with them *very* well.

"I don't need defending, you little sewer rat," Sue said. "Touch me again and you might lose a hand." To emphasize her point, Sharkey chomped her teeth a few times.

"I shall win my lady over in the end," Seth said.

"I'm *not* your lady," Sue said. "And I asked you a question."

"And I shall answer," Seth said. "I wear my underwear on the outside because it's the source of my powers, and I'm not afraid to show it. My underwear strikes fear in the hearts of my enemies!"

Tyrone snorted. "It also makes me want to give you the biggest wedgie of your life." Weasel thought that was hilarious, slapping her knees.

"And I shall face your wedgie with honor," Seth said. "I am no stranger to wedgies."

"Why do you keep saying, 'shall'?" Mike asked. "And talking like you're one of King Arthur's Knights of the Round Table?"

Seth blinked. "I was not aware of these accusations. I shall consider them and respond when the moon is big in the sky."

Nikki didn't know what that meant. Everyone else seemed confused too, scratching their heads and looking at each other. Except for Spencer, of course. He was never confused. "How many powers do you have, Seth—I mean, UnderMan?"

"Fourteen," Seth said.

"Urrrrrr!" Naomi growled. She blew out her breath in a huff. "*So* unfair. Why do all the Power Giver's minions get extra powers?"

"To protect the sanctity and honor of—" Seth started to respond, but George cut him off.

"To help run the Power Rankings. Otherwise all you power kids might destroy each other before you can finish your quest."

Nikki knew George was right. When George had appeared at the Taj Mahal, the Power Council and the Power Outlaws were about to destroy each other with their powers. "Thank you," Nikki said. "We really needed your help and you came through for us. It's nice to meet you, Seth—I mean, UnderMan."

"It is a pleasure to make your acquaintance, I'll be your guide on your quest," Seth said, bowing so low his nose almost touched the sand. "And welcome to the Power Island. Try not to die!"

Seth laughed crazily, and then turned around and walked away, his underwear as white as snow under the bright sun rising high in the sky.

7

Angry birds, poisoned arrows, and big, fat raindrops

Naomi was hot and sweaty. They'd been trudging through the jungle for what felt like hours. The weird thing was that the sun was still directly overhead, a ball of yellow flame staring down at them. It hadn't moved even a little bit, like the earth was no longer rotating on its axis.

But that wasn't the only weird thing. This jungle was odd in many ways. For one thing, she heard strange noises in the undergrowth, grunting and snorting and rustling. But every time she turned to see what was making the noise, she saw nothing. Occasionally birds flew over the trees, but they weren't normal birds. They were enormous and had beaks and eyes on *two* sides. It was like they were two birds joined together, complete with four wings facing opposite directions and four claws. All of the wings flapped at the same time, which sometimes made the birds fly one way and then back the other, as if they were unable to decide which way to go. Other times they would just spin in circles. Both beaks would *caw* and *caw* and *CAW!* until Naomi wanted to clamp her hands over her ears to block out the sound. She wondered what the freaky two-headed birds were saying.

The plants and trees weren't normal either. None of the leaves were green. And even the leaves that were autumn colors, like red and orange and yellow, were glowing. Naomi touched one and the bright blue leaf curled around her finger, clamping down hard, like a Chinese finger trap. "Ow!" she said. She tried to pull her finger away, but the leaf pulled back even harder.

"Relax your finger," a voice said from above.

Naomi looked up to find George sitting on a rainbow. "I don't need your help," she said.

He shrugged. "Suit yourself." Then he slid away, riding the rainbow further into the jungle. Naomi looked at the glowing leaf, then back at George and his rainbow. She wondered if George would tell the Power Giver about how she couldn't even beat a stupid leaf. Would she drop to number three in the Power Rankings? Would she drop even further?

Gritting her teeth, she relaxed her finger. To her surprise, the leaf released her, curling away from her skin. She smiled. Maybe this whole Power Island quest would be easier than she thought.

As she started walking again, another mosquito bit Naomi's arm. It was already her thousandth mosquito bite. Well, maybe her tenth or eleventh, but it *felt* like her thousandth. She slapped at her arm, but the mosquito was already gone. "I wish mosquito repellant was one of my powers," she muttered.

"Mosquitos?" Seth Powerundies said, walking over to her. "Why didn't you say something earlier? I've been on the Power Island for so long I've forgotten all about them."

"Go away," Naomi said. She knew it wasn't a very nice thing to say, but she couldn't help herself. She was just so hot, so tired, so mosquito-bitten, and *so angry.*

As usual, Seth didn't listen to her. She wondered if he had a hearing problem. Instead, he pointed down at his tighty-whities. The picture changed from the slingshot to a bug. That annoyed Naomi too. It wasn't fair that kids like George and Seth could change their powers so easily. That was one of *her* powers—no one else should be able to do it.

Something weird was happening to Seth. His entire body started glowing neon blue. His hands, his arms, his face…even his teeth! He looked like one of those bug zapper light bulbs that are sometimes hanging on buildings.

A buzzing sound filled the air. Naomi looked up to see a massive swarm of mosquitoes flying overhead. "Ah!" she yelled, covering her head. She was going to be eaten alive by mosquitoes!

Bzz! Bzz! Bzz! Bzz! BZZ!

There were a thousand more loud pops and crackles and buzzes, and when Naomi uncovered her head, the mosquitoes were gone. Seth had returned to his normal pale, skinny self, wearing that stupid grin of his.

"The mosquitoes will leave us alone for a while," Seth said.

Naomi was shocked. Most people didn't do nice things for her. She knew it was probably because she never did nice things for other people either, but Seth had helped her without asking for anything in return. "Uh, thanks," she said.

Seth nodded, bowed, and then continued onwards, leading the Power Team through the jungle. He tried to hold Sue's hand, but she shrieked and slapped him away.

Most of the other kids followed after Seth, ignoring her, but Naomi found Nikki Powergloves staring at her, smiling. "What are you smiling at?" Naomi said sharply. Nikki's smile vanished. That made Naomi smile.

Naomi wasn't on this quest to make friends. She wasn't on this quest to laugh and smile and be happy. Just like everything else in her life, she was doing this to *win*. Lifting her leg high, she stepped over a large purple root sticking out. Behind her, Slobber wasn't as nimble. He tripped on the root and fell flat on his face. Naomi sniggered, but helped him up. "Get up, you big oaf," she said, straining under his weight.

"Thanksh," Slobber said. He was a bit clumsy, and Naomi hated the way he drooled all over everything, but she knew she needed him. Slobber was the only one who hadn't abandoned her.

Up ahead, Sue was complaining to Seth. "Why do we have to trudge through this awful jungle? Why can't we just use our powers to get past it?"

Seth moved toward Sue to answer her, but Sharkey stepped between them. The sidekick opened her mouth wide, as if daring Seth to come any closer. Seth eyed Sharkey's sharp teeth and backed away. "The Power Giver makes the rules. I am just here to guide you on this quest."

Sue apparently wasn't satisfied with Seth's answer. "Yeah, but what if I were to switch my slippers like this"—Sue pulled out a pair of what Naomi thought were ridiculous-looking slippers, all covered in white feathers, and put them on her feet—"and then did this..." Huge bird wings shot from Sue's back, rising majestically over her head.

"I wouldn't do that," Seth cautioned.

"I'm done listening to you," Sue said, taking off into the sky, her wings flapping.

Naomi watched her go, curious as to whether she'd make it. At first she looked just fine, but then, suddenly, her wings stopped flapping. She hovered in midair for a second, but then her wings shriveled up and disappeared completely, and Sue fell from the sky, heavy as a rock. "Ahhhh!" she cried as she fell.

Seth ran underneath her. "I gotcha! I gotcha!" he yelled.

Sue crashed between branches and leaves, plummeting through the thick jungle foliage. When she was mere feet from slamming into the ground, Seth pointed his finger at the trees above and yelled something that Naomi couldn't understand. Something shot from his fingertip, wrapped around a tree branch, and collapsed on top of Sue as she fell. She bounced in the air once, twice, three times, and then came to rest. She was caught in a net, dangling from the tree branch.

"Get me out of here!" she shouted.

Naomi chuckled. Even when she'd been rescued by her gallant knight, Sue was still an obnoxious snob. What was even funnier was that her hair was all messy and tangled, and for once Sue didn't look quite as beautiful as usual.

"Right away, my lady!" Seth called, clambering up the tree and sliding down the rope to the net. Naomi was grudgingly impressed with how agile Captain Underpants was. He climbed almost as well as a monkey.

Seth fiddled with the net while Sue continued to scream at him, and then, all of a sudden, the net opened and they both fell the last few feet, crashing to the jungle floor in a tangle of arms and legs and Sue's ear-shattering shrieks.

"Bumbling half-wit," Sue muttered, pushing off Seth's stomach to get to her feet. He groaned. "What the heck happened up there?" she said when she'd regained her feet. "I was flying and then my wings stopped working."

"My guess is the golden clouds," Nikki's boy-genius sidekick said.

Usually Naomi was annoyed by everything that little know-it-all said, but this time her ears perked up. She gazed up at the sky. *The clouds,* she thought. *Are they really made of gold?* Gold was the one thing that prevented the power kids from using their powers.

The other little pipsqueak sidekick spoke up, agreeing with Spencer. "Yeah, that's got to be it! No one can use flying powers so long as the golden clouds are in the sky."

That certainly explained Sue's failed attempt at flight. *Interesting,* Naomi thought. *I'll have to find another way to get away from these kids.*

"We can't even fly? This quest is boring," Sue complained. "Except for Naomi getting her finger stuck in a leaf, nothing has happened at all!"

"I wasn't stuck," Naomi said. "I was just experimenting." Sue was starting to annoy Naomi even more than Seth or Nikki.

"Sure you were," Sue said, turning back. "Except you looked like you were about to cry."

"Was not!" Naomi said.

"Wah wah wah!" Sue said, rubbing her eyes and pretending to cry.

"Stop that!" Naomi said, feeling her blood start to boil. She changed her skirt to her turquoise one and a flock of pigeons appeared over her head. They had beady eyes and sharp beaks.

"You think your silly little birds scare me?" Sue said, changing into new slippers, brown moccasins. A bow and arrow appeared in Sue's hand. She pulled back the string and shot an arrow. One of Naomi's pigeons dropped to the ground, an arrow sticking out of its tail feathers. The bird immediately began snoring, put to sleep by some kind of poison in Sue's arrow. Sue laughed loudly. "Stupid birds."

"Stop it!" Nikki said, jumping between them with her hands out. Naomi immediately noticed her gloves, which were white with snowflakes painted on them.

Naomi wasn't about to listen to the girl who was ahead of her in the Power Rankings. "Pigeons! Attack!" Her pigeons burst forward, rocketing toward Nikki and Sue.

Nikki waved her white gloves and ice shot from her fingertips, coating the ground and then bursting upwards. Soon a wall of ice had formed between Naomi and Sue. Naomi's pigeons pecked at the wall with their sharp beaks, breaking off chunks of ice. Through the clear wall, Naomi could see Sue shooting her poisoned arrows into the ice. Each time one hit, more of the wall would crumble.

"Stop fighting!" Nikki cried. "We're the Power Team. You heard what George said. We have to work *together*."

But Naomi only joined the Power Team so she could find the Power Giver and win the prize. She suspected Sue was doing the same thing. So she kept attacking the wall with her pigeons, while Sue continued to shoot her arrows. Huge cracks were running up and down the wall, which looked like it was ready to shatter into a million pieces.

"STOP!" a loud voice boomed.

Naomi didn't stop, and neither did Sue, even when George stepped between them wearing clear glasses. The ice crumbled around him, showering over his head. Naomi's pigeons flew toward George. Sue shot her arrows at him. For once, they had the same idea: fight George.

Just before the birds and arrows reached George, a shadow loomed above them, blocking out the sun. Naomi looked up to see an enormous blob of...*what is that?* she wondered. *Oh my gosh, is that a—a raindrop?* The massive raindrop splashed down on Naomi's pigeons and Sue's arrows, washing them away in a flood of water. The water rushed between the trees and into the jungle, taking the pigeons and arrows with it.

Naomi glared at George. "I can make more pigeons, you know," she said.

"Don't," George warned.

Naomi raised her hand in the air.

"Don't," George repeated.

Naomi prepared to make more birds, thinking about wings and beaks and how funny it would be to see George covered in bird feathers.

But before her new flock of attack pigeons appeared, another gigantic raindrop fell, crashing onto her head and sweeping her feet out from under her. The powerful rush of water pushed her along, knocking her into the weird trees and the strange leaves, which tried to grab her. When she came to a stop, George was standing over her. "This is your first challenge. It was supposed to come later, but you and Sue made me start it earlier than I wanted to. Good luck."

George vanished, and big, fat raindrops filled the sky, falling from high above the jungle.

The golden clouds were gone, replaced by an ocean of black.

8

Clown car

Nikki didn't have time to be angry at Naomi and Sue for starting the fight. She was too busy running through the jungle, dodging gimungous raindrops created by George and his clear powerglasses.

SPLOOOSH! Another raindrop splashed down only a few feet away from Nikki. The water burst forward, rushing around her feet. She wobbled but kept her balance, taking high steps to gallop out of the water. All around her, other kids were running for their lives too. Just ahead, Freddy used his black and yellow socks to turn into a bumblebee. With the golden clouds gone, he zipped through the trees, but then flew right into a massive raindrop and fell to the jungle floor. Nearby, Britney used her green leaf earrings to transform into a leaf monster, but only ended up as a very wet pile of leaves. Samantha was doing a little better. She'd managed to use her yellow scarf to climb a large tree like a spider. But then the tree shook its branches like a wet dog and Samantha slid all the way to the ground, splashing into a deep muddy puddle. Nikki didn't even know where Mike, Tanya, or any of the sidekicks were. Axel, Tyrone, Naomi, Jimmy, and Sue were missing too.

A shadow loomed overhead. Nikki acted on instinct alone, pointing her white-gloved finger skywards and shooting a beam of ice directly into the giant raindrop. Instantly, the blob of rain became a huge ice ball, continuing to hurtle down toward her. "Yikes!" Nikki exclaimed, barely diving out of the way as the ice smashed into a million pieces beside her. *Ice power is no good against raindrops*, Nikki decided.

She was trying to figure out what to do next when she heard the revving of powerful engines. What she saw next was so out of place in the island jungle that Nikki had to open and close her eyes a few times to make sure she wasn't dreaming. A sleek yellow Ferrari roared down the trail, spraying water and mud.

"Who is that?" Nikki wondered out loud.

As the beautiful car skidded to a stop, Axel stuck his head out the window. He was wearing a stylish yellow racing jacket. "Get in!" he shouted. The car door opened straight up, like some kind of futuristic rocket car.

Nikki didn't need a second invitation. She dove inside, bumping into someone as the door lowered behind her. She heard the spray of mud and the Ferrari rocketed forward, throwing her against the backseat. Well, it wasn't really a "backseat," more like a shelf to put groceries. The good news was she was a kid, and sort of small. The bad news was that there were three other kids stuffed into the back with her. Chilly Weathers was curled into a ball and muttering, "No place like home, no place like home..." Dexter Chan had one foot tangled with Nikki's arm, and the other tangled with Chilly's leg. And Spencer was grinning at Nikki and singing "Giant raindrops keep falling on my heeeeaaaaddddd!"

Beside Axel in the front was Mike, shouting out instructions. "Left, left, left!" Mike ordered.

"There are too many trees to the left!" Axel shouted back.

"It's a jungle, there are trees everywhere!" Mike said.

Axel turned left, the side of the car scraping the trunk of a tree as Nikki felt the rear fishtail back and forth. Through the rain-spattered windshield, Nikki saw Samantha, Britney, and Freddy huddled together. They were all soaking wet and slimy with mud. Axel hit the accelerator and the car sprung toward their friends.

"Giant raindrops keep falling on my HEEEEAAAADDDD!" Spencer crooned.

As it turns out, Spencer's song was almost like a prophecy, because just then the biggest raindrop yet landed right in front of the Ferrari.

"Riiiiiiiiiiight!" Mike shouted, but Axel was already spinning the wheel hard to the right. A mountain of water slammed into the side of the car. Nikki, Chilly and Dexter all screamed while Spencer kept singing and the car rocked onto two wheels.

"Hold on!" Axel shouted, but Nikki was already clutching someone's arm and the back of Axel's seat. For a moment it felt like the Ferrari might topple over, but then Axel expertly spun the wheel to the left and the car slammed back onto four wheels. Once more, he skidded to a stop, pressed a button to open the door, and shouted, "C'mon c'mon c'mon!"

Samantha, Freddy and Britney piled in, somehow squeezing into a vehicle that was already full to capacity. Nikki wondered if this was how sardines felt.

"GO!" Mike yelled, and Axel propelled the car through the jungle. It was the scariest few minutes of Nikki's life as branches whipped against the windows, Axel jerked them left and right, dodging raindrops, and water sprayed all around them, making it impossible to see through the glass.

But then, with a final burst of speed, they shot into a wide clearing and sunlight shone all around them. Axel eased to a stop and let out a deep breath. "Well, that was fun," he said.

"Not for me," Chilly said, her voice muffled. "Someone's butt is in my face."

"Sorry!" Dexter called. "I can't seem to move."

For the next few minutes, they untangled themselves from the car, eventually falling out into the jungle clearing, which was surprisingly dry. It was like the giant raindrops had never existed at all. Everyone thanked Axel for the ride and complimented him on his awesome car, even if it was dented, scratched, and muddier than a pig in a sty.

"Where's everyone else?" Nikki eventually wondered aloud.

"There!" Spencer pointed at the sky.

In the jungle behind them, huge drops of rain continued to fall. Amongst the fat blue drops was an even bigger orange balloon. "Is that a…hot air balloon?" Nikki asked.

"Yeah, but look, it has a face," Dexter said.

"Not just any face," Mike added.

"It's Tanya!" they all said at the same time. Tanya Powershirts had become a hot air balloon, her skin stretched out like a blimp, her body filled up with helium. Her feet had become a large basket, and there were kids inside it.

"Tyrone and Weasel!" Britney exclaimed.

Something else caught Nikki's attention. "Oh no," she said, "he's not going to make it."

"Who?" Chilly asked.

"Jimmy." She pointed at the sky near Tanya the Hot Air Balloon. Sure enough, Jimmy was wearing his rocket boots and soaring through the air, ducking and diving and dodging the raindrops. The closer he got to the clearing, the thicker the rain became. Nearby, the raindrops were bouncing off of Blimp Tanya, who was protecting Tyrone and his sidekick.

Nikki gasped as a ball of water slammed into Jimmy. He spun in the air, the fire in his rocket boots sputtering out and coughing up thick black smoke. "Ahhh!" he yelled as he fell from the sky.

With surprising quickness, Tanya steered herself to the side and under Jimmy. He crashed on top of the balloon, bouncing twice before coming to rest on his back. When Tanya landed in the clearing, Nikki and her friends rushed over. Tyrone and Weasel leaped out of the basket while Spider Samantha clambered up the side to check on Jimmy.

Nikki held her breath, hoping he would be okay. Ten seconds later, Samantha called, "He'll be fine!" and Nikki exhaled.

Tanya began to deflate, the massive balloon billowing out to the sides and eventually settling on the ground like a parachute. Samantha and Jimmy clambered off and then Tanya morphed back into herself.

Tyrone, Weasel and Jimmy approached her. "Thanks, Tanya," Tyrone said, extending his hand.

Tanya slapped it. "You're welcome," she said.

Weasel gave her a high five, too, and then handed Tanya a dollar. "Sorry, I stole it from you when we were playing on the beach."

Nikki shook her head. Weasel really needed to learn not to steal things from people, even if she was very good at it.

Jimmy was the last to say something. He was drenched from head to toe, rainwater dripping from his nose and earlobes. "I…" he said, scuffing his rocket boots against the ground. "Why did you save me?" he asked.

Tanya bit her lip. She looked really unsure of herself, as if all the attention was embarrassing her. Nikki didn't think Tanya looked ugly at all anymore. Maybe she never did. She wondered if people only saw what they wanted to see sometimes. Tanya said, "Because I think you're cool. And I think you deserve another chance at facing the Power Island. But mostly I just didn't want to lose a member of the Power Team."

Jimmy looked stunned. "I—that's the nicest thing anyone has ever said to me."

"I meant every word," Tanya said. She didn't look embarrassed anymore. She was smiling a very pretty smile.

Spencer said, "Jimmy, I think I know why you almost didn't make it."

Jimmy nodded. "I know why, too. I tried to beat the raindrop challenge alone. I should've been a part of the team. I'm sorry. I screwed up."

Nikki stepped forward. This was a different Jimmy than before. He wasn't a villain. He wasn't even a bad kid. He was a superhero, a team member, and a friend. "It's okay," she said. "Just learn from your mistakes and we'll all help each other next time."

"I will," Jimmy said.

"Not to be a downer," Tyrone said. "But we're still missing a lot of kids, and the golden clouds are back so we can't use flying powers."

Nikki realized he was right. Above them the clouds were painted with gold, and outside of the clearing, the huge raindrops continued to fall. Naomi, Slobber, Sue, Sharkey, and Peter were nowhere to be found.

Even worse, Seth Powerundies and George Powerglasses were gone too. They were stuck in the middle of the jungle without a guide.

9

CRYBABY!

Sue hated to admit it, but without Peter Powerhats and his monster truck, she might've never escaped from the giant raindrops. The only good thing was that Naomi and Slobber wouldn't have made it either. They had tried everything before Peter came roaring up, his massive tires chewing through the mud and dirt. Sue had become Robo-Sue, but the rain had fried her electrical circuits. She'd even tried her ballet slippers so she could be more graceful, but her wet clothing had dragged her back down into the mud. Naomi had attempted to skateboard away, but her wheels got stuck in the muck. And when she turned into an ogre, the mud only caked around her feet faster, making her sink into the soft ground.

Peter had saved them, even if he was too dense to realize it.

Now they roared from the jungle into a large clearing, and Peter slammed on the brakes. Slobber and Naomi, who weren't holding on tight enough, flew from the monster truck and skidded across the ground. Sharkey clamped her teeth around the doorframe and managed to hang on, while Sue used her ballet slippers to jump gracefully from the truck and land softly on her feet.

"Did you have a nice trip?" she said to Naomi and Slobber.

Naomi spat dirt from her mouth. "Hilarious," she muttered.

"Sorry!" Peter said, hopping down. He was wearing his blue hat with the big wheels on the side. "I'm good at driving, but not at stopping."

"Doofus," Naomi said.

"That doofus saved you," Sue pointed out, "maybe you should be a little nicer to him."

"Thank you, goober," Naomi said to Peter.

He scratched his head. "You're welcome?"

Sue shook her head. "You might be talented with your powers, but you couldn't charm a puppy."

"Oh yeah?" Naomi said. "Who needs to charm a puppy when you can kick one?"

Sharkey gasped and Slobber's mouth dropped open. Even Peter seemed shocked. Only the meanest of people would kick a sweet little puppy. "Glad you're finally showing your true colors," Sue said.

Naomi turned bright red. "It just slipped out...I was so angry and I wasn't thinking and...I would never...I swear...I would never actually kick a puppy."

"You sure about that?" Sue asked. It was fun seeing Naomi squirm and get all embarrassed.

"Yes, I mean, I think so," Naomi said. Sue frowned. She'd never seen Naomi look so uncomfortable. She was hanging her head and looking at her feet.

Sue felt a little bad. Or at least a smidgen bad. Maybe just a pinch. "Hey, I'm sorry, I wasn't trying to get you all upset."

She took a step toward Naomi, but the dark-haired girl recoiled away from her. "I'm fine. It's nothing." She kicked at the dirt. "Peter, I'm sorry I called you a goober. And a doofus. Thank you for saving us. You were awesome back there."

50

Peter smiled a big goofy smile and said, "I drived really good."

"Uh, yeah, something like that," Naomi said.

Sharkey said, "I think he meant *I drove really well*." Sue laughed. She didn't realize her sidekick was the grammar police.

"Anywayyy," Slobber said, wiping a line of drool off his chin. "Where are we? We need to find the resht of the Power Team."

"No," Sue and Naomi said at the same time. Sometimes it scared Sue that she was so similar to Naomi.

"We should create our own Power Team," Naomi said. "Just the five of us. We'll find the Power Giver on our own and win the ultimate prize."

Sue rolled her eyes. She had to admit, Naomi was pretty good at making speeches. Too bad she didn't mean any of it. "Ha! You mean *you* will win the ultimate prize. I know exactly what you're doing. You're trying to use us to find the Power Giver so you can trick us and win the Power Rankings."

Naomi glared at her. "As if you're not trying to do the exact same thing!" Sue blinked, surprised that Naomi had seen through her beauty pageant act. Naomi imitated Sue's high gentle voice. "Oh, please, I would love to be on the Power Team. I just want to be friends with you, Nikki Powergloves! We can hold hands and tell each other stories! Together we can win! Together we can defeat evil! Blah blah blah!"

"I do NOT sound like that!" Sue screeched, sounding almost exactly the way Naomi had imitated her. She cringed at her own voice. "Okay, fine, Ms. Smarty Pants. I want to win. So what? What's wrong with winning? It's fun. But maybe we CAN work together to get to the end, and then we'll see who's the best superhero." Sue liked her idea. They'd stand a better chance working together anyway.

"Fine," Naomi said, crossing her arms. "But I'll beat you in the end."

"Maybe, maybe not," Sue said.

"This is all a very bad idea," a voice said from above. They all looked up to find George on the back of his purple-winged Pegasus.

"You should go find the rest of the Power Team. You have to work together or you'll never cross the island."

"Leave us alone," Naomi said. Sue almost laughed—it was exactly what she was about to say.

"Suit yourself," George said, flying away.

As they watched him go, Sue heard a wet squishing sound. "My ladies and sirs!" a voice crooned. They turned around just as a huge ball of undies rolled up to them. Water dripped from the white fabric, forming a puddle around it.

"Oh gosh," Naomi said. "This day keeps getting weirder and weirder."

"Weird is my middle name!" Seth sang from somewhere inside the ball of underwear.

"I thought your middle name was danger," Sharkey said. Sue giggled at her sidekick. She never knew she had such a good memory.

Seth's head popped out of the soggy undies. He grinned. "I have been called by many middle names," he said. "Danger, Weird, Bony Butt...even Jorge!"

"Yeah, well, that's good to know," Sue said. "Good luck with whatever you're doing in that wet ball of undies, but we've got to get going."

"I know," Seth said, pulling one arm, and then the other, out of the ball. "I'm coming with you. I'm your guide, remember? I'll help you find the rest of the Power Team."

Sue blew her hair away from her face. "We already told George, we don't need you. Go help the others, or roll around, or do whatever it is that you do on this island."

"But my lady—"

"GO!" Sue shouted.

Seth's face fell and his lip quivered. *Oh gosh,* Sue thought as a tear trickled from the corner of Seth's eye. *This kid is so annoying!* "Don't be such a crybaby," she said, turning away from him. "C'mon. Let's go." She stalked across the clearing, heading for the other side of the jungle.

At first she didn't think the others would follow, but then, one by one, she heard their footsteps behind her. *Good*, she thought. *We have no room on our team for crybabies anyway.* She refused to turn around and look back at Seth.

When she was more than halfway across the clearing, thunder boomed overhead. *Oh no, not again*, she thought. "No more rain," she muttered.

But when the sky thundered again, it wasn't a boom as much as a loud voice:

"CRYBABY!" the voice rumbled.

Startled, Sue looked up. The others had caught up and were staring at the sky too. "What the heck?" Naomi said.

"Is that a…?" Sharkey said, trailing off.

"It'sh sho big," Slobber said.

"I wish I had a giant hamburger," Peter said. "I love onions on hamburgers."

Sue ignored them all, too focused on the massive onion hovering in the sky. It was the size of a cloud, floating lazily over them. A dark line formed along one of the curved sides, and part of the onion began to peel away. "Oh no," she breathed.

"The onion is slicing itself!" Naomi shouted. "Take cover!"

They ran back the way they'd come, the hot island breeze sticking their wet clothing to their skin. "Ruuuuuuun!" Sue yelled as she felt the cool shade of the onion slice's shadow surround her.

She took two more giant steps and then dove as gracefully as a ballet dancer, executing a perfect roll and coming back onto her feet.

BOOOOOOM! The ground beneath her feet rumbled as the onion slice hit the earth.

"AHHHH!" a boy screamed. Sue spun around, her eyes widening as she took in the scene. The biggest onion slice she'd ever seen was resting in the clearing, the bright sun reflecting off droplets of moisture on its white coat. Peter Powerhats was screaming, grabbing at his ankle.

53

"It landed on my leg! I wanted it on a hamburger, but it landed on my leg!" Big fat tears rolled down his cheeks.

Naomi was nearby, slapping her knees and laughing. "Have you ever seen someone trapped under an onion? Hilarious!" However, soon her laughter turned to tears, streaming down her face and dripping off her chin. "What the heck?" she sobbed.

Sue realized her own eyes were stinging too. The air was filled with the pungent aroma of chopped onions. Sue remembered how when she watched her dad chop onions it would sometimes make her eyes water. It was like that now, her vision blurring, clouded by tears.

Slobber was crying, too, his tears combining with the drool already running down his chin. "Shomeone needsh to help Peter!" he cried.

"Not me," Naomi blubbered, wiping away tears as fast as they dribbled from her eyes.

Through her tears, Sue glared at her. "He *saved* us before! The least you could do is help him now."

At first Naomi just crossed her arms, staring at Peter, who was still clutching his leg and screaming. Finally, she uncrossed her arms and said, "Fine. Let's get him out of here."

Together, the four kids worked to get Peter out. Sharkey chewed through as much of the onion as she could, spitting out white chunks as she went. Slobber drooled all over Peter's leg to make his skin slippery so they could pull him out. "Gross!" Peter cried. Naomi turned back into an ogre and used her strength to lift the onion a few inches off of Peter. Sue grabbed Peter under the arms and pulled him out the moment the onion was high enough.

"It hurts!" Peter sobbed.

Sue blinked away her tears and inspected his leg. His ankle was badly bruised and swollen. It looked like he had a tennis ball stuck under his skin. "Do you think you can walk?" she asked. They were all still crying, which made it hard to talk and even harder to see.

"I'll need help," Peter said, rubbing his eyes.

"I'll help," Slobber said, grabbing Peter's arm and pulling him to his feet.

"Thanks," Peter said. He roped an arm around Slobber's back, leaning on him.

"You're *my* sidekick," Naomi said, transforming back into a girl. "You'll only help Peter if I say you can help him."

Sue rolled her eyes. "Seriously? You sound like a dictator. Peter can't even walk."

"Slobber, I give you permission to help Peter," Naomi said.

"Uh, thanks," Slobber said.

"Yeah, thanks," Peter added.

"You're such a saint," Sue said sarcastically.

Naomi ignored her. "Now we need to get away from this onion so we can stop crying," she said.

Sue couldn't argue with that. "That way," she said, pointing back at where Seth's head was still sticking out of his ball of undies. He wasn't crying anymore, which meant the onion's smell didn't reach all the way to him.

While Slobber helped Peter hobble toward Seth, the rest of the kids ran across the clearing. When they arrived at Seth and his undie ball, he said, "Are you ready for me to lead you back to the rest of the Power Team?"

"Yes," Sue said at the same time that Naomi said, "No."

The two girls stood facing each other, nose to nose. "We need a guide," Sue said.

"Yes, but we don't need the rest of the Power Team," Naomi argued.

"CRYBABY!" the voice in the sky boomed, louder than a thunderclap.

"Look what you did!" Sue shrieked. Another line was forming in the onion, cutting off another slice.

"Alas, you have angered the Power Giver," Seth said.

"That's who's doing this?" Naomi said. "Why won't he leave us alone?"

"Because you've failed to follow his rules. You must work together as a team. The Power Team. If you do not, his wrath shall be upon you."

"Dude, why do you talk so weird?" Sharkey asked.

"I do not know," Seth answered.

"Who cares?" Sue said, glancing skywards. The next giant onion slice was peeling away from the rest of the onion, teetering on its edge. "We've got to run!"

"How can we stop the onion?" Naomi asked.

"The onion shall only stop following you when you rejoin the rest of the Power Team," Seth said.

Sue knew they had to listen to UnderMan. They had no other choice. "Lead us," Sue said. She turned to Naomi. "Agreed?"

Naomi nodded, her cheeks tearstained.

"Follow me, young superheroes!" Seth cried, rolling away. "Leave no kid behind!"

Naomi started to rush after Seth, but Sue grabbed her arm. "We need to help Slobber with Peter," she said, even as a giant onion shadow cast them into darkness.

"They'll catch up," Naomi said.

"Only if we help them," Sue said, squeezing harder. "Please."

Naomi let out a low growl. "Fine," she said.

Together, they went back for Peter, who was far behind, still leaning on Slobber's shoulder. "I got this," Naomi said, transforming back into the ogre. She hefted Peter up onto one shoulder as if he weighed no more than a feather, and stomped away, her footsteps rumbling.

Shocked, Sue smiled, surprised at the rare display of kindness from Naomi. Maybe she wasn't so bad after all. It almost made Sue want to be a little nicer, too. Almost.

10

Two more sleeps before powers go bye-bye

Nikki was having trouble deciding whose side she was on. Freddy and Mike wanted to go look for Seth, because he was the only guide they had for the island. Samantha and Britney thought they should continue on through the jungle. Jimmy, Tanya and Tyrone wanted to go back to find Peter, Naomi, and Sue, because they might be hurt or lost. The sidekicks had stuck with their superheroes, leaving only Nikki and Axel and their sidekicks in the middle.

"What do you think?" Axel asked June the Goon.

Nikki was impressed. She never thought Axel would care about anyone's opinion except his own. June said, "We're supposed to do this as a team, right?"

Spencer nodded quickly. "Remember the black and white *yin yang* Weebles?"

Of course. Nikki would never forget them. Even if Naomi was really mean sometimes, she was now part of their team, as were Peter,

Sue and their sidekicks. But Seth was also part of their team, in a way. He was a little strange and talked funny, but he'd already helped them get this far through the jungle. They couldn't just leave him behind.

"We have to go back," Nikki said. "Not just for Seth, but for the others. Maybe for George, too, although I don't think he needs our help."

As it turns out, George appeared overhead at that exact moment, surfing on one of his rainbows. "Very good," he said. "The Power Giver approves. Updated Power Rankings!"

George and his rainbow vanished and were replaced by a list of names, written with white, puffy clouds:

1. Sue Powerslippers
2. Nikki Powergloves
3. Peter Powerhats
4. Mike Powerscarves
5. Tanya Powershirts

Nikki was shocked. Not only had she fallen from #1 to #2, but she was replaced by Sue Powerslippers! Sue must've done something really awesome and really good to have gained the #1 spot in the Power Rankings. And Naomi wasn't even in the top 5 anymore, which meant she'd been doing a lot of bad stuff.

"I can't believe—there must be a mistake—I didn't expect..." Tanya was having trouble getting her words out.

"Congratulations," Nikki said to Tanya. "You made the top 5. She patted her on the back.

"Thanks," Tanya said. "Wow. I never thought I'd make it."

They two girls smiled at each other. "You deserve it," Nikki said. "That hot air balloon move was amazing."

Everyone was congratulating Nikki, Mike, and Tanya, and discussing how Sue and Peter moved so far up the rankings.

Everyone except Spencer, who Nikki noticed was looking off into the distance. Spencer said, "That's weird."

Nikki joined Spencer. "What's weird?" All she saw was a big white cloud moving their way. It really stood out next to all the golden ones. It was shaped like a half circle.

"Watch," Spencer said. "Parts of that cloud keep falling off."

Nikki stared at the cloud, trying not to blink. "Oh yeah!" she said when another slice of cloud tumbled away, dropping into the jungle. The ground rumbled slightly under her feet as the cloud landed amongst the trees. "What do you think that's all about?"

"I think we're about to find out," Spencer said. The cloud was moving closer and closer, and getting smaller and smaller as slices of it tumbled from its sides.

There was a loud cracking sound as a tree splintered on the edge of the clearing. A big white ball of soggy underwear rolled from the jungle. Just behind it stomped a huge creature, with green, warty skin and big red lips. It was wearing a green skirt.

"Seth? Naomi?" Nikki said.

"RAAAAAAR!" Naomi the Ogre bellowed, stomping toward them. Big green tears were sliding down her cheeks. She was carrying a large boy wearing a blue hat. Peter Powerhats! He was also crying. Just behind Naomi and Peter were the rest of the missing Power Team: Sue, Sharkey, and Slobber. The three of them were bawling, but Nikki couldn't seem to figure out why.

A shadow fell over Naomi and the others as they ran toward them. *The oddly shaped white cloud is following them*, Nikki realized. Another slice fell off and landed with a deafening crash just behind them, which only made the group cry even more.

"Onions!" Spencer yelled, figuring it out a moment before Nikki. She could smell them now, the pungent odor stinging her eyes. Now she felt like crying too!

"NIKKI!" Naomi the Ogre growled. "GRAB MY HAND!"

It was a very unusual thing for Naomi to say, but Nikki didn't question it. Somehow she knew it was important. Tears sprouting from her eyes, Nikki charged toward the big, green ogre, reaching out. Above them, she saw the rest of the onion cloud tumble toward her.

She knew she was about to be squashed, but still she reached for Naomi, who reached for her. The onion was moments away from hitting them, but then their fingers met. Naomi's rough, green, ogre hands touched Nikki's nine-year-old girl hands, and there was a flash of white light.

Nikki blinked, clearing her vision. She no longer felt like crying. She looked up. The onion cloud was gone. Further along the clearing, the other onion slice had disappeared too, as if it never existed.

"Look!" Samantha said, running over to Nikki and pointing at the sky. The Power Rankings had changed once more:

1. Naomi Powerskirts
2. Nikki Powergloves
3. Sue Powerslippers
4. Mike Powerscarves
5. Tanya Powershirts

"You're #1," Nikki murmured at the ogre.

"WHAT?" the ogre bellowed. "I AM?" Naomi changed back into herself, staring at the sky. "I did it! I'm #1!" Naomi grabbed Nikki and pulled her into a hug.

"Uh, congratulations," Nikki said. She didn't feel very happy for Naomi, but it seemed like the right thing to say, especially because Naomi had saved Peter and also helped stop the onions from falling.

Naomi seemed to realize she was hugging Nikki and froze. She pushed her away, a look of disgust on her face. "I can't believe you're still #2," Naomi said, looking at Nikki as if she was a slimy worm.

"Thanks a lot," Nikki said, turning away. She didn't want to be near Naomi for another second. She was the meanest girl she'd ever met.

"I'm catching up to you, Nikki," Sue said. She approached Nikki, walking with dainty, graceful steps and flashing a white, straight smile.

"Good job," Nikki said, not really meaning it. She was surrounded by ex-Power Outlaws who only seemed to care about winning the Power Rankings.

Spencer put his arm around Nikki and steered her away from Naomi and Sue. "Don't worry about them," he whispered. "All that matters is staying together and finding the Power Giver."

For the millionth time, Nikki felt lucky to have Spencer as her sidekick and best friend. "You're right," she said.

"Of course I am," Spencer said, grinning.

Nikki grinned back, and then located the rest of their friends, who were inspecting the giant ball of wet underwear. Mike tapped on the outside. His knuckles squished on the waterlogged material. "Seth?" he said.

A head popped out and Mike leapt back, startled. "Ah, I see we have escaped the onion and been reunited with our stalwart companions," Seth said. "My ladies and sirs, your first day is over. You must sleep now, for on the morrow you shall surely face even greater challenges than today."

"Sleep?" Samantha said. "But it's still daytime. It's still sunny." Her forehead was crinkled in a frown of confusion.

"The sun hasn't moved even the littlest bit since we arrived on the Power Island," Spencer said. Nikki gazed at the sky. She knew Spencer was correct. The sun was high in the sky, hot and clear, just as it had been on the beach, hours earlier.

"You are mistaken, young sidekick," Seth said. "Night is upon us and sleep beckons."

At that very moment, the sun fell from the sky like a shooting star, sinking all the way to the horizon. There was a loud sizzling sound, like bacon on a fry pan, and a burst of steam shot into the air.

"Um, I think the sun just went for a swim," Freddy said.

"You don't see that every day!" Dexter said excitedly.

"It's like the greatest magic trick ever," Chilly agreed.

Darkness fell so fast it was as if a huge black blanket had been thrown over the earth. There were no lights, no torches. Nikki could barely see her friends through the murk. She couldn't help feeling a little scared, out here in the middle of a jungle. Who knew what creatures might only come out at night in a wild place like this?

"Find a spot to rest and close your eyes," Seth instructed. "You will find that sleep comes easy, so long as the thousand-eyed glow worms do not nibble your toes off!"

Britney whimpered and grabbed Nikki's hand. "Is he being serious?" she whispered.

Nikki had no idea if half of what Seth said was serious. All she knew was that she suddenly felt exhausted, like she might fall asleep standing up if she didn't find a place to lie down. "I doubt it," she said to Britney, to comfort her.

As all the kids lay down in the grass for the night, Nikki remembered what Naomi had said to her before they started this journey, something about sleeping with one eye open. For a while Nikki tried to, but eventually her eye closed.

Just before she drifted away to dreamland, she heard Spencer say, "Two more sleeps before powers go bye-bye." The world faded.

11

Nighttime Weeble rodeo

Nikki was having a nice, peaceful dream about clouds that were like marshmallows, as soft as pillows and sweet as sugar.

Her beautiful dream was smashed away by the sound of a loud gong, resonating through the quiet night. She gasped as, all around her, fiery torches burst to life. Somehow, she remembered Seth's warning about the thousand-eyed worms, so the first thing she did was check that all ten of her toes were still there. She breathed a deep sigh of relief when they were.

The next thing she did was look around her. The rest of the Power Team was waking up one by one as the gong continued to clang.

"What's happening?" Samantha asked, scooting over to Nikki's side.

Britney was huddled against her other side, clutching her arm. "Are the natives attacking?" Britney asked.

"I don't think so..." Nikki murmured.

Spencer's voice rang out high and clear. "Weebles," he said. "I see Weebles!"

"Don't feed them after midnight," Tanya muttered, rubbing her eyes.

Nikki peered through the gloom. Sure enough, scampering amongst the shadows cast by the torches, she caught glimpses of beaver tails and the flash of porcupine quills. Then they were gone. The sound of hundreds of feet scurrying through the grass was like a ghostly whisper.

Above them, the stars were shining so brightly they were like spotlights. The moon was ten times its normal size, a huge old man's face in the dark sky. As the stars began to move, Nikki said, "Oooh." The rest of the kids were *ooh*ing and *ahh*ing, too, watching as the stars began spelling out names and rankings. Soon the same Power Rankings as the day before lit up the night sky, with Naomi at #1 and Nikki at #2.

Naomi's voice called out above the sound of scuttling Weeble feet. "I'm number one! I'm number one!"

Nikki's fists tightened at her sides. She couldn't let someone like Naomi win the Power Rankings! Whatever challenge they were about to face, she had to win it.

"Hey, y'all!" a familiar voice said. "It's high time fer a Power Team showdown!" The small, black Great Weeble rolled into the center of the power kids. "This is all y'all's chance to show the Power Giver just how good ya are. Win the rodeo and you'll be one step closer ta winnin' the greatest prize ya ever seen."

"Rodeo?" Spencer said, looking around. "I don't see any bulls."

Nikki had been to many rodeos. It was a favorite pastime back home in Cragglyville. Twice a month, all the locals would head over to watch the best riders, ropers, and horsemen and horsewomen try their luck against the nastiest bulls and wiliest steers in town.

"This ain't yer every day rodeo," the Great Weeble said. "This here's a Weeble rodeo! Now choose yer mounts!"

Twelve Weebles rolled out from the gloom. They were the biggest Weebles Nikki had ever seen, not including the Weebles that had been fed after midnight and turned into giants. These Weebles were snorting and pawing at the ground, almost like real bulls. They were wearing saddles, but no ropes or reigns, which meant the kids would have to cling to their porcupine quills in order to ride them.

Despite his injured foot, Peter Powerhats was the first to make a move, hobbling over to one of the bull Weebles and jumping on. The white brown-spotted Weeble immediately started bucking and leaping as thousands of Weebles crowded around on all sides, cheering. Less than three seconds later, Peter was tossed in the air. "Boooooo!" the Weebles groaned.

"I got him, I got him!" Slobber shouted, his arms outstretched to catch Peter. Peter landed hard on the grass a few feet away from Slobber. "I don't got him," Slobber said. Slobber and Sharkey pulled Peter off to the side to rest his leg.

Next, Mike pushed past Nikki, Britney and Samantha. "I can do this," he said. He hopped onto a large red bull Weeble and slapped it on the rump. "Ride 'em Weeble!" he cried. "Yeehaw!"

Despite his confidence, Mike's ride didn't last long either, maybe one second longer than Peter's. Mike ended up dirty and bruised in the grass, with Weebles booing and taunting him. "You stink like a football player's socks!" one of the Weebles shouted.

"How'd I do?" Mike asked, ignoring the Weebles. He pulled himself to his feet.

As if in response to his question, the night sky lit up. A fiery comet streaked across the sky and the stars began reforming the Power Rankings. Mike's name disappeared, Tanya's moved up to #4, and Samantha's name popped up in the 5th spot, leaving the Power Rankings looking like this:

1. Naomi Powerskirts
2. Nikki Powergloves
3. Sue Powerslippers
4. Tanya Powershirts
5. Samantha Powerbelts

"Sorry, Mike," Samantha said. "I guess the Power Giver wasn't too impressed."

"Darn!" Mike said. "I'm glad it's you who moved up though."

Nikki was glad too. In her opinion, Samantha deserved to be in the top five. She only wished Naomi and Sue would fall off the star leaderboard.

Someone tapped Nikki on the shoulder and she turned around. It was Spencer, and he was standing on his tiptoes to whisper in her ear. "Use your powers," he said. "Woot woot!"

It was such an obvious suggestion, and yet none of the other kids had thought of it yet. Sometimes Spencer could just see what other kids couldn't. Tyrone was about to make the same mistake, having jumped on one of the smaller bull Weebles, a yellow one with blue stripes. He clung to its quills as it twisted and jerked around. The Weebles cheered in excitement. About five seconds later he tumbled to the ground, rolling twice before stopping. He shook his head, dazed, and then said, "Those bulls are harder to ride than my brother's Harley Davidson motorcycle!" His sidekick, Weasel, helped him up. Nikki glanced at the sky, but the rankings hadn't changed. Apparently Tyrone's ride wasn't good enough to move him into the top five.

Thinking about Spencer's advice, Nikki moved to the back of the group of power kids. Spencer followed her. When no one else was looking, she opened her powerchest. "Which powers are you going to choose?" Spencer asked.

"How about you pick one and I pick one?" she said.

"Really?" Spencer said.

"Of course." Nikki put her arm around Spencer's shoulders. "You're my sidekick. I trust you more than anyone."

Spencer nodded. He licked his lips and then began humming softly to himself, considering which of her powers might be the best for riding a bull Weeble. "You could use your plant-growing glove to grow some vines and then tie yourself to the Weeble," Spencer said. "But I think the bull would just break them." Spencer hummed for another ten seconds and then snapped his fingers. "I bet seeing the future would help you!" he exclaimed.

"Great idea, Spence!" Nikki said, snatching her pink tarot card glove from the chest.

Next Nikki considered which other glove to choose, eventually deciding on her purple super-strength glove. Wearing it, her fingers would be stronger and she'd be able to hang on tighter. With her two gloves, Nikki already felt more confident.

When they returned to the group of power kids, Britney had just climbed onto one of the bull Weebles. She was so light that the Weeble didn't even realize she was there for a second, allowing her to gain a few seconds' advantage. But that edge was soon lost when the bull Weeble noticed her, immediately tossing her off. Seth Powerundies appeared out of nowhere and managed to dive underneath her. A big white trampoline burst from his back and Britney bounced on it a few times before coming to rest safely.

"Thanks," she said as she climbed off. That's when Nikki realized that the big white trampoline was actually just his underwear stretched out really tight. It was another one of his powers! As the underwear snapped back to normal size like a rubber band, Nikki and her friends giggled. Seth's powers were pretty cool, but also pretty funny.

"Seth, Seth, he's the best! And his undies stretch farther than all the rest!" the Weebles sang, which only made the power kids laugh harder.

"I was just doing my duty," Seth said with a low bow. "The only reward I ask is a kiss."

"Eww!" Sue blurted. "I'd rather kiss my hairy Uncle Bob."

Although Nikki didn't say it, she wouldn't have really wanted to kiss Seth either. Or Sue's hairy Uncle Bob. But Seth's eyes were already closed and his lips puckered. Britney looked around, trying to decide what to do, and then grabbed Seth's arm, kissing him on the back of his hand.

Seth's eyes flashed open in surprise, and he said, "I can die happily now." He fell over into the grass and pretended to be dead. Britney blushed and rejoined her friends. Together they looked at the sky, but the rankings didn't change. Britney's ride wasn't good enough either.

Nikki started to take a step forward, but Spencer said, "Wait a little longer." She nodded and watched as Sue, Freddy, Tanya, and Jimmy all tried riding one of the bull Weebles. Out of the three, Sue lasted the longest, but none of them rode for more than five seconds. The Power Rankings didn't change at all, and the Weebles booed and booed until Nikki could barely hear herself think.

Nikki looked at Spencer and he nodded. "Good luck, Cowgirl!" he said.

Nikki slapped her hands together and marched out into the center of the kids.

"Number one Nikki! Number one Nikki" the Weebles chanted.

"I'm number one! I'm number one!" Naomi shouted in response. She elbowed Slobber in the ribs and he joined in her cheer.

"She'sh number one! She'sh number one!" he cried.

Nikki did her best to ignore the commotion all around her, focusing on the rodeo. There were only four bulls left to choose from. From some of the rodeos she'd been to, she knew that the smallest bulls weren't always the gentlest ones. She picked the second smallest, a Weeble with pink stripes on white quills, because it was the only one that didn't look like it wanted to eat her.

"Good girl," she said, approaching the Weeble with her gloved hands out.

The Weeble responded in a deep New York accent. "Hey, kid, you think just because I wear pink I'm a girl? Men can wear pink too!"

"Pink is cool! Pink is cool!" the other Weebles sang.

Oh boy, Nikki thought. *I'm not doing too well.*

"Sorry," she said. "You're right."

"No offense taken," the bull Weeble said. "But just because you apologized doesn't mean I'm going to take it easy on you."

"Crush her! Crush her!" the Weebles cheered.

Nikki cringed. "I know," she said, swallowing a thick knot in her throat. She took a deep breath and then jumped onto the Weeble's saddle.

The Weeble began bucking immediately, throwing its hips into the air. Using her super-strength, Nikki clung to its quills for dear life. She also dug her heels into the bull's sides to keep her balance. But the Weeble was too strong and Nikki felt her grip start to slip. It was time to use the glove Spencer had picked out. In her mind, she pictured a crystal ball and tried to visualize what the bull Weeble would do next. She saw it toss its head to the left, to the right, and then twist in a circle, kicking out its legs in the front and back.

She blinked and the image disappeared, reality returning. Now that she knew what the bull was going to do, she was ready for it. Nikki didn't try to fight the Weeble, but instead became one with it, like the bull was an extension of her own body. She let it pull her left and right and up and down. To her surprise, Nikki actually started to enjoy the ride!

As she rode, she continued to use her powers to see ahead to what the Weeble would do next, until it finally stopped bucking and thrashing and slowed to a stop. "Well done, Nikki," the bull said. The Weebles cheered.

Nikki stopped thinking about the future and let down her guard. That's exactly when the Weeble bucked one more time, as hard as it could. Nikki's hands and feet slipped away and she tumbled through the air. She twisted in midair and landed on her super-strong feet.

The Weebles cheered even louder, this time for the clever bull who found a way to throw her off. Everyone on the Power Team surrounded her, patting her on the back and congratulating her on a good ride. Well, everyone except Sue, who was still sulking about her own failed ride, and Naomi, who had her powerchest open and was rummaging through it.

"Great job, Nikks!" Spencer said.

"Thanks, but I never would've thought of using my powers without your help." Spencer beamed as a comet flashed in the sky. The stars moved and the rankings changed! Nikki and Naomi swapped positions, with Nikki once more in the #1 spot!

"HOORAY!" Spencer cheered.

They turned back to the rodeo, where only three bulls remained. Samantha strode out, wearing her white belt. She jumped on the first Weeble she came to, which happened to be the smallest one. Nikki didn't know whether it was a smart move or not.

The bull raced across the clearing and then stopped suddenly, trying to toss Samantha over its head. Samantha didn't budge. "Sticky sticky sticky!" Spencer crooned.

Nikki remembered the Samantha's white belt gave her the power to shoot sticky gum-like stuff from her fingers. That's how she was hanging on—she'd actually stuck herself to the Weeble! Nikki grinned, proud of her friend. Above them, the rankings were already changing. As she clung to her bull, Samantha moved from #5 to #4 to #3 to #2. She was going to pass Nikki!

That's when the bull made a brilliant move. It dove to the ground, rolling in the grass. Sticky stuff sprayed from Samantha's fingers, going everywhere, hitting the ground. For a moment she was stuck to the Weeble and the ground, but then the bull managed to pull itself loose, leaving Samantha covered in gum. "Heh heh heh," the Weeble laughed, galloping away.

Still, it was an amazing ride, and all the kids surrounded Samantha to congratulate her. Even Sue stopped by to say, "Good job," which really surprised Nikki. She wondered if Sue was being fake nice or real nice. It was hard to tell with that girl.

Next up was Axel, who used his beige cloth jacket to create a cow stampede. The cows surrounded the bull he was riding, until the Weeble could hardly move. Axel's trick worked for a while, but eventually he lost control of the stampede, and the cows started bumping him and the bull. "Hey, watch it!" Axel shouted, but it was too late. The cows knocked them over.

When Axel got up and dusted himself off, the stars had already changed the Power Rankings. Axel was #5, knocking Tanya off the leaderboard. Most of the kids gave Axel high-fives and back slaps, but his sidekick, June the Goon, gave him a big hug. At first Axel went all stiff, but then he hugged her back. "I told you," June said. "You're a superhero whether you like it or not."

Axel played it cool, pretending her words meant nothing, but Nikki could tell he was trying not to smile.

Last up was Naomi. She was wearing a determined expression and her pink and black striped skirt with the picture of the skateboard on it. Nikki knew it was a mean thing to think, but she hoped Naomi fell off her bull quickly.

The last bull Weeble was the biggest of all, snorting and stamping and shaking its head. "You should give up now," the Weeble said.

The rest of the Weebles chanted, "Give up! Give up!"

Nikki didn't know what she would do in Naomi's situation. She hoped that she would face the challenge, but it would be hard with such an angry-looking bull in front of her. Nikki couldn't help but to admire the way Naomi didn't show any fear or hesitation. Instead, she marched right up to the bull and said, "You're the one who should give up." Then she jumped on the Weeble's back, but not like how the other power kids did. Instead of sitting on it with both legs hanging down the sides, she stood on the saddle with her arms out. She looked more like a skateboarder or surfer than a bull rider!

It was a risky maneuver, Nikki knew, but as soon as the Weeble began to move, Nikki could tell Naomi had made an incredibly smart decision. No matter how fast the bull ran, or how hard it bucked, Naomi kept her balance like a pro.

"She looks…amazing," Britney said beside her, clearly in awe of what she was witnessing.

In truth, Nikki felt the same way, even though she hated to admit it. Naomi was the best cowgirl of all. After ten minutes of the bull Weeble trying every trick in the angry-bull book, it gave up, bowing its head in surrender.

Naomi hopped down and raised her hands in victory. "Eat that, suckers!" she said, pointing at each of the power kids. Then she pointed at the sky, where the rankings had changed one more time:

1. Naomi Powerskirts
2. Nikki Powergloves
3. Samantha Powerbelts
4. Sue Powerslippers
5. Axel Powerjackets

"Get over here, Slobber," Naomi said. Obediently, Slobber walked over. Naomi jumped into his arms and forced him to parade her around the clearing. Grudgingly, the other kids were forced to congratulate her. Nikki wished Naomi wasn't such a mean winner. That might make it easier to be happy for her. Instead, Nikki secretly hoped Slobber would trip over and drop her.

Nikki felt bad even thinking such an awful thing, but she couldn't help it. It was like Naomi had forgotten to get in line when they were handing out hearts in heaven, leaving her with only an empty black hole inside her chest.

When the Naomi Parade was over, Nikki yawned. She was exhausted. All she wanted to do was go back to sleep and rest for the next day.

Before she could lie down, however, Seth clapped his hands and said, "Hear ye, hear ye! Rise and shine, for we now begin another day on the Power Island. Keep your wits about you, for today will be even harder than yesterday."

"But it's still dark," Freddy complained.

"Behold, the morn comes on chariots of ice!" Seth declared.

12

Sun to snow and fire to ice

The sun burst from the horizon, and immediately everything changed. The air went from hot and muggy to cold and icy. The tropical palms transformed into snowy evergreens. Beneath them, the grass was frost-covered, crunching under their feet. Snow began to fall in big lazy flakes as gray mist surrounded them. The only thing that hadn't changed were the golden clouds, which continued to float by overhead.

"Um, what just happened?" Dexter asked, catching a snowflake on his tongue.

"The island moved," Spencer said. "Remember what George said before? The reason no one has ever discovered the Power Island is because it keeps moving around. Let me guess, we went from the Caribbean to the North Pole?"

"Good guess, young squire," Seth said, pulling his tighty whities up to his bellybutton. "First we were close to Hawaii, and now we're near the top of a mountain in Antarctica."

Nikki shivered. It certainly felt like Antarctica. Wearing only her shorts and a t-shirt, she'd freeze to death out here.

"Step up to the line, boys and girls," Seth said, clapping his hands. Nikki blinked. Seth was now dressed in thick layers, complete with gloves, a hat, and a long white cloak that resembled a cape. In fact, everything he wore was white, and seemed to be made out of—

"UnderMan!" Spencer exclaimed.

Seth laughed and nodded.

"One of your powers?" Spencer asked.

"Yep," Seth said, pointing to the white underwear he was still wearing on the outside of all of his other clothing. There was a drawing of a shirt and trousers on them. "I can make clothing out of underwear material with just a snap of my fingers. Well, technically I don't even have to snap my fingers, I can just think about the clothing I want and it just sort of appears, or comes into existence, or—"

"We don't care *how* it happens," Naomi interrupted. "Are you going to give us some warmer clothes or not?"

Although Naomi said it in a very mean way, Nikki was thinking the same thing. She couldn't last much longer in this cold. Each breath misted in the air, as if all the warmth she had left was leaving her body.

"Of course, of course," Seth said. "My sincerest apologies, my fair maiden. As the current leader in the Power Rankings you may have the first....that is to say, you are entitled to receive a nice selection of gear that includes, among other things—"

"Just give it to me!" Naomi snapped, snatching a bundle of clothing from Seth's arms. She immediately began pulling a white shirt over her head, right on top of her summer clothes.

Nikki's teeth chattered. "My lady," Seth said, handing her another bundle.

"Sp-Sp-Spencer first," Nikki said, passing it to Spencer, who was starting to turn blue.

"Th-th-thanks," Spencer said, too old to even come up with a nickname for her.

Seth once more tried to give Nikki a bundle of clothing, but then she had a thought. "G-Give them to all the others f-first. Everyone, ggather around." Nikki pulled out her powerchest and opened it. Her fingers were so numb from the cold that she had trouble gripping the gloves that she wanted. Eventually, however, she managed to slip her hands inside. The gloves she'd chosen looked even brighter red next to the snowy landscape.

She thought fiery thoughts, and a flame appeared from one of her fingers. Nikki could feel the warmth through her gloves, but it didn't burn her. Concentrating, she made the flame grow bigger and bigger, crackling between her hands, roaring into a fireball.

The kids cheered, huddling around her, putting their hands out to warm their skin. Sharkey opened her mouth wide, as if to warm her teeth. Spencer, already half-dressed in Seth's undie-clothing, turned around and stuck his butt out. "Ahhh," he murmured. "That's the good stuff."

Nikki giggled, and her teeth didn't even chatter. She felt toasty all over, and she was still wearing her shorts and t-shirt. She couldn't wait to bundle up in the clothing Seth made.

"Rightly done, fair maiden," Seth said, continuing to hand out bundles of clothes. Each time he got rid of one, another appeared in his arms. Nikki smiled, and then placed the fireball on the ground. It immediately melted the snow into a puddle, and then dried the puddle.

Mike, who was already fully dressed in Seth's warm clothes, also had his green scarf wrapped around his neck and shoulders. "Who wants a marshmallow?" he said, his hands suddenly full of fluffy, white, sugary treats.

"Me me me!" the kids said. Britney and Samantha went to gather some sticks, and soon everyone was roasting marshmallows by the fire. Mike got even more creative, using his scarf to make graham crackers and chocolate so the kids could make s'mores. Axel requested a hotdog, and moments later was heating it up next to the flames. From there, all kinds of requests came in, until the kids were full and warm and in relatively good spirits considering the icy weather.

While the kids chatted and ate, Nikki finally got around to examining the clothes Seth had given her. According to Seth, the kids were to put them on from the top of the pile to the bottom. The first item was a funny-looking body suit with buttons in the middle. *Long underwear*, Nikki realized. It even had footies at the bottom to keep her feet warm. She stepped into the underwear, which fit her perfectly and clung tight to her skin. The material bunched a little around her shorts, but it wasn't too bad. Next she pulled the top of the underwear over her head and stuck her arms into the sleeves. Spencer helped her fasten the buttons, which were in the back. From there she added three shirts and three pairs of pants, each thicker than the previous one. Next came warm socks, a hat, and even a scarf. No one except Seth got a cape. He was UnderMan, after all.

When she was finished, it was kind of hard for Nikki to move her arms and legs, but at least she was warm and protected against the snow.

The only thing left were Seth's gloves. To wear them, she'd have to remove her red powergloves. "Sorry guys," she said. "We'll lose the fire for a minute, but then it'll be back."

There were groans of dismay as Nikki slipped off her powergloves and the fire disappeared with only a wisp of smoke to prove it had ever been there in the first place. She quickly pulled on the white gloves, and then replaced her powergloves, and soon the fire was going again. The kids cheered and danced and enjoyed the warmth.

A comet flared across the snowy sky. White numbers and letters appeared. Nikki thought they looked like they were formed from snow. The Power Rankings! Nikki gasped as she realized she was once again in first place!

"What?" Naomi shrieked. "But she didn't even *do* anything except make a little fire."

There was a loud *pop!* and a flash of bright light and George appeared, wearing his yellow sunburst glasses. He looked at Naomi.

"You're a smart girl. You'll figure it out." There was another *bang!* and a flash and George was gone once more.

"That dude comes and goes faster than a monkey riding a motorcycle," Tyrone said.

Nikki let out a surprised laugh. She never knew Tyrone could be so funny. Come to think of it, she didn't really know him at all.

Spencer whispered in her ear. "I think I know what George meant by what he said to Naomi."

Nikki wasn't surprised at all. "You should tell the whole group," Nikki said. They were supposed to be one team, the Power Team, so they shouldn't keep secrets.

Spencer hummed, thinking about it, and then nodded. "You're right. Hey everyone!" Spencer clapped his hands to get the group's attention. All the kids had split into groups and were discussing the new Power Rankings.

"What do you want, Braniac?" Naomi said, hands on her hips.

Spencer smiled a big, toothy smile. "I know why Nikki is back in first place," he said.

"So do I," Naomi said. "It's because the Power Giver favors her. This whole competition is completely unfair."

Spencer shook his head. "Not if you know the rules. From the day we met George Powerglasses, he told us we have to stop fighting and work together as a team, right?"

"So what?" Naomi said. "We are working together. We're here, aren't we?"

"Just being here isn't enough," Spencer said. "The Power Giver wants us to really help each other. Yeah, he gives us points for using our powers well. For example, Naomi, you were awesome during the Weeble rodeo. Not just awesome...the best of all of us."

Naomi took a step back, as if shocked by the compliment. "Uh, I know....I mean, thanks. Yeah, thanks."

"I'm just speaking the truth," Spencer said. "So the Power Giver gave you a bunch of points for winning that challenge and you moved into first. But Nikki got even more points for helping everyone get warm by using her fire power. And did anyone notice who else moved into the top five."

Everyone looked up at the sky except Mike, who was grinning. "Me," he said. "I didn't want to say anything, but I'm #4 now."

"Whoa! Nice job, Mike," Chilly said. Samantha patted him on the back.

"But all he did was give out a bunch of food," Naomi complained.

"Exactly," Spencer said. "That was something that helped all of us. Food makes us stronger as a group. The Power Giver must've given him a bunch of points for doing that for us."

"This is so stupid," Naomi said, stamping her feet. "I was amazing in the rodeo, you said it yourself, boy genius. I should be first."

Nikki was starting to get even more annoyed at Naomi. Why couldn't she just listen to what Spencer was saying? She was about to say something when Sue stepped forward. "He's right," Sue said. Nikki was shocked. Most of the time, Sue was every bit as mean and nasty as Naomi, even if she hid it under a pretty smile and sugar-sweet words.

"I am?" Spencer said. He seemed to be as surprised as Nikki.

"He is?" Naomi echoed.

"Yes," Sue said. "We don't make the rules, but if we want to win, we have to follow them. It's your choice, Naomi."

"Whatever," Naomi said, and stalked off. "Slobber!" she called behind her. Slobber, like an obedient puppy, followed after her, a line of frozen drool running from his lips to his chin.

"Where are you going?" Samantha asked. "We have to stick together."

"I don't need you screw-ups," Naomi said. "I'll prove you all wrong. I'll find the Power Giver and win the ultimate prize all on my own."

With that, she and her sidekick disappeared into the snowstorm.

To everyone's surprise, Peter Powerhats limped after her. "I'm comingggg toooo!" he crowed.

13

The real opposite day

They'd been trudging through the snowy forest for a long time, and Britney's legs were starting to feel like lead. There was snow caked all over her shoes, making them heavier and heavier with each step.

Luckily, she had a power she could use to help her. She got out her black dangly earrings and clasped them to her ears. A moment later she felt as light-footed as a fairy. Well, technically she *was* a fairy, complete with a pixie wand and light-as-air fairy feet that didn't sink into the snow at all.

"Cool!" Tanya said beside her.

Britney smiled shyly. She didn't really like to have attention on her, but she liked Tanya. Tanya was shy and quiet like her. Britney waved her pixie wand and pointed it at Tanya's feet, which were sunk deep into the snow. Tanya's eyes widened as her feet slowly rose out of the snow and rested on top.

"I—I feel so light!" Tanya exclaimed. "Thank you so much!"

"Well done, fair princess," Seth said. He was having no trouble walking through the snow, because he was wearing snowshoes made out of undies strapped in the middle of thick branches that had been tied together.

The rest of the kids gathered around. Some of them had been using their powers already. Nikki, for example, had been doing her best to use her fire power to melt some of the snow so it would be easier for all the kids to walk through the forest. Even still, the snow was falling so fast that she couldn't melt it all. Samantha had been using her green belt to make the trees come alive, moving out of their way so they could walk in a straight line. Freddy was digging holes and pushing the snow into them. Jimmy Powerboots volunteered to be their scout. He would teleport a little ways ahead and make sure nothing dangerous was waiting for them. Axel was wearing his white sweatshirt, which gave him skis and poles that allowed him to skim over the snow with June the Goon on his back. They were a great team.

However, some of the other kids, especially the sidekicks, didn't have any powers that would help them against the snowdrifts. And without being able to use flying powers because of the golden clouds, they were stuck fighting for every step. As they stood in a line, Britney used her pixie stick to make each of them light on their feet, so they could run on top of the snow.

When she was finished with Spencer, Dexter, and Chilly, they started dancing on the snow. "C'mon Sharkey and Weasel! You next!" Spencer said.

Sharkey and Weasel looked at each other and shrugged. Britney aimed her pixie stick at each of them and cast her spell. Soon they were dancing right beside the other sidekicks. Sharkey kept opening and closing her mouth like she wanted to bite someone, but instead she started eating the snow.

"Watch out for yellow snow!" Spencer said, laughing.

"I think you mean watch out for snowballs!" Weasel exclaimed, launching a snowball at Spencer.

"Ninja quickness!" he declared, trying to dive out of the way. It smacked him in the back of the head and knocked him off his feet.

Everyone laughed, even Spencer.

When Britney was finished casting her spells, there was a flash of light in the sky and the Power Rankings appeared. "What?" Britney said aloud.

A sixth spot was now dangling beneath the top five kids. It looked like this:

1. Nikki Powergloves
2. Naomi Powerskirts
3. Samantha Powerbelts
4. Sue Powerslippers
5. Mike Powerscarves
6. Britney Powerearrings

"Cool!" Freddy said. "You're in the rankings now, Britney!"

Britney blinked twice to make sure she wasn't seeing things. Sure enough, she was still ranked #6.

"It's because you helped some of us," Chilly said. "You earned it."

Despite the cold, Britney felt her face begin to warm. She'd never won anything, or even come in second. She was always very…average. In school she got B's and C's. In soccer she got to play sometimes, but she never scored any goals. Even on the Power Council, she was more of a follower than a leader. Even though she was only #6 now, it still felt like she'd won. "Thanks," Britney said, staring at her shoes.

"This just proves what Spencer said earlier," Samantha said. "If we work as a team, we get more points."

"But there can still only be one winner," Sue pointed out. "And that someone is going to be me."

Britney wasn't about to argue with Sue. In truth, Sue reminded her of the really pretty girls at her school. They always scared Britney a little, because of how confident they were. Britney never felt very confident.

Thankfully, Seth said, "We should keep moving. The rankings will change even more now, as you complete each challenge and work as a team. Follow me."

Britney let out a deep sigh of relief as the kids continued walking. She was glad to have the attention off of her once more. Inside, however, she was doing cartwheels. *I'm #6!* she kept thinking to herself.

Because of Britney's help, they were all able to move a lot quicker now, and soon the forest began to thin out around them. There were fewer trees and bushes, and more rolling hills and drifts of snow.

Up ahead, Jimmy called out. "I found something!"

Britney's heart started beating faster in her chest. He could mean anything. It could be a treasure, or something really dangerous or scary. But during training, Nikki had taught Britney how to handle her nerves. She stopped for a second, taking deep breaths. As Nikki had instructed her, she thought only positive thoughts. She thought about all the friends she had made. She thought about all the times she'd used her powers to do good and amazing things. Soon the fear left her and she was smiling. Whatever Jimmy had found, they would face it together as a team.

On fairy legs, she hustled to catch up to the others. Her smile vanished as she saw what Jimmy had found.

"What *is* that?" she asked.

"A line," Spencer said, grinning. For a second she thought he was making fun of her, but then he winked and she knew he was joking.

Of course, it *was* a line. Or at least she thought it was. There was a blue stripe in the snow in front of them, running to each side. Britney gazed in one direction. She couldn't see where the line ended, if it ended at all. The same was true in the opposite direction, where the line seemed to go on forever.

"What does it mean?" Nikki asked.

"Maybe we can't cross it or something bad will happen," Britney suggested. Despite her deep breaths and positive thinking earlier, she was having trouble controlling her thoughts. She pictured them stepping over the line and the ground breaking underneath them.

Seth said, "It's nothing *too* bad."

Somehow that didn't comfort Britney because it still meant something bad might happen.

Sue stepped up to the line, her toes practically touching it. "It's just a line," she said. "We shouldn't be scared of a line."

Britney couldn't help but to admire Sue for her courage. Even if she was a little mean sometimes, there were a lot of good things about her too.

Sue started to take a step, but Sharkey grabbed her arm. "Are you sure you want to do this?" Sharkey asked. "We could try to go around."

Sue rolled her eyes. "You guys are being ridiculous." She shrugged away from Sharkey and stepped forward.

Britney held her breath, feeling her heart beat loudly in her chest. Nothing happened. Sue turned around. "It really hurts," she said.

Britney frowned. It didn't look like Sue was in any pain. Her face was calm. She was even smiling. "I mean, it hurts so much!" Sue exclaimed, much louder this time. Her smile got even bigger.

Something weird was going on. If Sue was joking, it wasn't a very funny joke.

"We've got to help her," Tyrone said, striding forward over the line. He looked like he tried to grab Sue's arm, but instead he grabbed her leg.

Sue smiled a big smile at him and swung a hand like she was going to slap him, but instead she cupped his cheek in her palm and rubbed his face gently.

Spencer started humming, Sharkey said, "Weird," and Nikki jumped over the line. Nikki grabbed at Sue and Tyrone, and Britney thought she was trying to push them back over the blue line, but instead she started pulling them further past it.

"Nikki, what are you doing?" Samantha asked. Britney was wondering the same thing.

"I'm not trying to help them," Nikki said.

"*Not* trying to help them?" Axel said. "Don't you mean you *are* trying to help them?"

Nikki shook her head. "No, I mean *not* trying."

Axel raised an eyebrow. "She's not acting like herself," he said. Britney agreed. Nikki was one of the most helpful kids she'd ever met.

Spencer stopped humming. "Opposite day," he murmured.

"What did you say, Spence?" Dexter asked.

"Have you ever played that silly game where you say it's opposite day?" Spencer asked the group.

Britney knew exactly what he meant. She didn't really like that game, but some of the kids at school did. It was where everything you said and did on a certain day was actually the opposite from what you really meant. *Yes* meant *no* and *no* meant *yes* and *of course* meant *no way!*

"Yes!" all the kids on their side of the line said at the same time. On the other side of the line, Sue, Nikki, and Tyrone all said, "No!"

Oh boy, Britney thought. *This is serious.*

"See what I mean?" Spencer said. "That's why they're acting so weird over there. Everything they're doing and saying is the opposite of what they really want to do and say."

Even now, Nikki, Sue and Tyrone were walking further and further away from them, which meant that they were trying to come back. And they were smiling the whole time, which really meant they were frowning on the inside.

"Welcome to the *real* opposite day," Seth said. "This is your next challenge, ladies and sirs. Make it to the other blue line and you'll be one step closer to finding the Power Giver!" With that, Seth sprouted springs on the bottom of his feet and bounced across the line after Nikki and the others.

"Although it makes me want to throw up just saying it, I should've gone with Naomi," Sue said.

Spencer shook his head. "This challenge isn't as hard as you might think. All we have to do is think and do the opposite of what we really want to do, so that we do the opposite of the opposite of what we actually want to do."

"Um," Axel said. "I think you just made my brain explode."

"Let me try to explain it better," Spencer said. "Once I'm across that blue line, if I want to chase after Nikki, I have to think about running away from her, and force my legs to run in the *opposite* direction. That way this weird island will force me to run right toward her. Make sense?"

Britney nodded. It *did* make sense. Something important popped into her head, and she couldn't stop herself from blurting it out. "We should choose our powers now, because it will be hard to pick the right ones once we're across that line." Everyone stared at her and she felt the heat of the blush on her cheeks.

"Great idea!" Spencer said. A few of the others nodded and smiled at her. Britney looked at her feet.

"We have to hurry," Samantha said. "They're getting further and further away." Britney gazed into the distance, where even Tyrone looked as small as a mouse.

There was a rush of activity as the power kids selected their powers. A horde of monkeys surrounded Freddy when he slipped on his fuzzy brown socks. Axel turned into a giant orange. June jumped up and balanced on top of him. Jimmy cloned himself at least a dozen times. All the Jimmys started talking at once. Tanya transformed into a sleek red convertible. She revved the engine, and Spencer, Dexter, Chilly, Weasel and Sharkey jumped inside, squashed like sardines in a tin can. Samantha used her peach belt to grow four additional legs and two more arms. Mike was now made of rubber, bouncing up and down on his butt.

Britney stared inside her powerchest, trying to decide what power to choose. She had no idea what might help them in the challenge ahead. "C'mon!" Spencer shouted, urging her to hurry. Frantically, she grabbed the first pair of earrings she saw, the red heart ones. She fumbled at the clasps and managed to slide them through the tiny holes in her ears.

As each of the kids stepped or rolled up to the blue line, Samantha said, "Remember what Spencer said. It's *opposite day* over there. We have to think and do the opposite of what we really mean to think and do, right?" With that, everyone crossed the line.

14

I love you! Mwah mwah mwah!

Nikki didn't know what was going on. At first she'd tried to help Sue and Tyrone. But when she wanted to push them back across the line, her arms had disobeyed her, pulling them further away. Then she tried to run back to safety, but instead her legs took her away from her friends. When she tried to stop altogether, she ran even faster.

Tyrone and Sue seemed to be having the same problem. The weird thing was that they were all grinning at each other like idiots. Nikki tried harder and harder to frown, but her lips only pulled upwards into an even bigger smile.

She knew she needed to use her powers, but every time she attempted to pull out her powerchest, her hand got stuck in her pocket, jamming the chest further inside.

"We need to get away from the others," Nikki said to Sue and Tyrone. *What? No!* That's not what she wanted to say.

"Yes, we do," Sue agreed. Tyrone nodded, still smiling like a fool.

What was happening to them? Nikki wondered. Up ahead, a gray mountain climbed into the golden clouds. She wanted to squint, to take a closer look at the mountain, but instead her eyes widened and her neck twisted around, forcing her to look back. It was like her body was doing the opposite of what she wanted it to do.

That's it! she realized. They were in some strange mixed up part of the island where everything was the opposite of what you wanted it to be. As she was thinking about that, she was still looking back, and that's when she saw her friends coming. Samantha had grown extra arms and legs and was leading the charge. Just behind her were a dozen Jimmys and a horde of monkeys led by Freddy. Tanya was a car full of sidekicks, and Mike was made of rubber, bouncing along beside her.

"Keep going!" Nikki yelled to Tyrone and Sue, when what she really wanted to say was "Stop!" *Argh!* she thought. *This is SO frustrating.* She tried to calm her breathing, which only made her breaths come shorter and faster. When she tried to gulp down the saliva in her mouth, instead she spit it on the ground.

Think, think, think! she urged herself. *What would Spencer do?* She could almost hear his voice in her head, telling her to "Think and do the opposite of what you mean to!" She realized that she *could* hear his voice, because he was shouting from the back of Convertible Tanya.

His words made sense in a strange, twisted way, but it was SO HARD to think the opposite of what you really wanted. Still, she had to try. *Run faster, run faster, RUN FASTER!* she thought to herself. Her feet slid across the snowy plain, but then she finally came to a stop. When she tried to look at Spencer and the rest of the Power Team, she turned and looked at the mountain instead. *Think opposite,* she reminded herself. She forced herself to try to look at the mountain so that she would turn around and look at her friends.

Some of them were having trouble with Spencer's instructions. The Jimmys were running in circles. Freddy's monkeys were pulling and biting each other's tails. Convertible Tanya skidded to a stop and the sidekicks tumbled out into the snow. Samantha tried to catch them with her extra arms, but instead hugged herself. Axel the Giant Orange couldn't seem to figure out left from right and was zigzagging through the snow, jerking back and forth so fast that June the Goon tumbled off. Britney was standing completely still, watching the melee with a big goofy smile that looked nothing like her normal pretty smile.

Somehow, Sue and Tyrone had managed to turn around and come back, and now they had their powerchests open. Nikki knew exactly how they had managed it. *Do NOT open my powerchest*, Nikki thought. To her delight, she was finally able to pull out her chest and open it in the snow.

Nearby, Sue had changed into her silver metal slippers and morphed into Robo-Sue. Tyrone was wearing a thin gold necklace and pounding his fist into his palm. They were both grinning like hyenas. Nikki wondered whether they had managed to choose the powers they really wanted, or if the island had made them choose different ones.

Nikki tried to concentrate on her own powers. Being able to grow plants might help her. If she could grow some long vines, she might be able to grab a few of the kids who were having trouble with opposite day. However, when she tried to grab her green gloves, her fingers went straight for her black and yellow ones! *No!* she thought as she closed her chest and slipped on the wrong gloves.

But it was too late. She couldn't control her thoughts, which were trying NOT to use the black and gold gloves to control the weather. Of course, it was opposite day, so the more she tried NOT to do something, the more she did it. Dark clouds smothered the golden ones overhead. Snow began falling faster and harder, collecting around her feet. All Nikki could think about was the beautiful sunny weather from the day before, which only made the storm even worse, until she could barely see anything.

All she knew was that something really bad was happening. The monkeys were screeching. A gang of Jimmys bolted past, tripping her. Robo-Sue stomped past, almost squashing her. Tyrone gave chase, swinging a big fist at Sue. The impact was like a car crash and Robo-Sue went flying. It was the power of Tyrone's thin gold necklace—a super-punch! Tanya the Convertible was driving in circles, doing donuts in the snow. The sidekicks were running around, almost getting hit by the car. Samantha was swinging her many arms and legs at anything that moved. Rubber Mike was bouncing off of monkeys and Jimmys, knocking them over like bowling pins.

Above all the chaos, Spencer was shouting, "Think and do the OPPOSITE of what you really want to do!" But if anyone heard his message, they were having a lot of trouble following his advice.

And because of Nikki, the snowstorm continued to rage around them.

That's when Nikki saw Britney. She walked calmly between the others, a look of determination on her face. Her red heart earrings seemed to shine with fire. When she tugged on them with her fingers, red sparkling lights shot outwards, spiraling around the kids. A bunch of the sparkles collected around Nikki's ankles and then began moving upwards, covering her skin. Despite the cold, warmth filled her skin and bones, nestling deep into her heart. The other kids were covered in red sparkles, too, all of them back to being just kids, not cars and oranges and clones and monkey-herders. As Nikki looked around, she felt one very very powerful emotion…

Love.

She couldn't help herself. She loved them. All of them. She loved Samantha and Britney and Mike and Freddy and Axel and June and Tanya and Dexter and Chilly and Tyrone and Weasel and Jimmy. She even loved Sue and Sharkey. Although she knew she loved some of the kids on the Power Team, she never realized she loved *all* of them.

Apparently the others were feeling something similar, because Spencer was running around yelling, "I love you!" to anyone he could find. Then he would kiss them on the cheek a few times—"Mwah! Mwah! Mwah!"—and move on to the next kid.

"I love you too, Spence," Nikki said when he came to her. And even though it felt wet and gross when he kissed her, she loved that too.

Britney, meanwhile, was hustling around, grabbing kids by the arms and pulling them close together.

"Group hug!" Sue shouted, grabbing Nikki and Spencer. Sue squeezed them tight. Nikki squeezed back. "I love you guys!" Sue exclaimed.

"Everyone get in a line," Britney instructed.

"Can we put our arms around each other?" Mike asked. "Please please, pretty please!"

"Yes, that would actually help," Britney said.

The kids formed in a line and Nikki put her arms around Spencer on one side and Sue on the other. While Britney urged them to walk forwards, Spencer kept kissing Nikki's hand. *Blech*, she thought. "Again," she said, and he kissed her again.

Together, in a line of huggers and kissers, the kids moved forward, marching toward the gray mountain. With Britney pushing them onwards, they crossed a blue line in the snow. It looked really familiar as Nikki stepped over it.

All of sudden, the red sparkles disappeared from her skin and the warmth melted from her chest. An icy wind slapped against her face. Spencer's lips were on her hand, wet and slimy. "Gross, Spence!" she said, pulling away.

Spencer looked stunned, his lips still puckered. "Why was I doing that?" he asked. "I couldn't seem to stop myself."

The other kids were equally confused. "I can't believe I hugged Sharkey!" Weasel said. "I can't believe I hugged Weasel!" Sharkey replied.

"Why did I keep saying I loved all of you?" Sue asked anyone who was listening. "I don't even like any of you."

Britney was the only one not talking. She cleared her throat with a soft cough. "Shhh!" Spencer said. "Britney has something to say."

Britney scuffed her shoes in the snow. "I, well, I just thought that maybe, you know, if I used my red heart earrings, I might, well, I thought—"

"It's okay," Nikki said, approaching her. "Just tell us. We won't be mad."

Britney took a deep breath. "I gave you all a love potion," she blurted out.

"You did *what?*" Sue said, her breath coming out in a warm white cloud. Her fists clenched and she stomped forward.

Nikki stepped in front of Sue. "Don't," she said. "Britney was only trying to help."

"No," Spencer said. "She *did* help. She saved us from ourselves."

Britney was looking at her feet, but managed a shy smile.

"Yeah," Mike agreed. "She made us stop running around in opposite-land like crazy people. She made us love each other so she could get us to safety."

Samantha was nodding. "We beat the challenge because of her," she said.

"I've still got genius drool on my cheeks because of her," Sue muttered, but no one was really listening. They were all too busy surrounding Britney and thanking her.

Nikki gave her friend a pat on the back and then noticed a lone tree standing nearby. Huge icicles were forming beneath its branches. They seemed to be spelling out something. "The Power Rankings!" Nikki exclaimed when she realized what she was seeing. The kids gathered around to look:

1. Britney Powerearrings
2. Nikki Powergloves
3. Samantha Powerbelts
4. Naomi Powerskirts
5. Sue Powerslippers
6. Mike Powerscarves
7. Tanya Powershirts

"Britney! You're #1!" Nikki said. She gave her friend a hug. Britney's real smile was back, more beautiful than a sunbeam.

"I—I don't know what to say," Britney said. "I've never been first at anything."

"Well now you have," Nikki said. "Great job. You saved us."

Nikki noticed Spencer scanning the icicles. "Now there are seven spots," he pointed out.

"More and more kids are getting ranked," Samantha said. "I think that's a good thing."

Nikki agreed. *Maybe it's because we're working as a team*, she thought.

The kids gathered around and congratulated Britney, as well as the other kids who were in the Power Rankings. *The only ranked kid who is missing is Naomi*, Nikki noticed.

Before Nikki could think too much about it, Seth reappeared, stepping from behind the tree. "Congratulations on defeating the opposite day challenge," he said. "Now get some rest, tomorrow is your last day to find the Power Giver."

"What, are we just supposed to sleep in the snow?" Sue asked.

"Of course not, my lady," Seth said. He stuck his thumb in his mouth and pushed out a breath, like he was blowing up a balloon. His underwear burst outwards, filling with air and growing bigger and bigger, until it was a huge white tent, surrounding them all.

"An undie house!" Spencer said gleefully. Only Spencer would get excited about camping out inside a giant underwear tent.

Nikki peeked outside the only opening to the tent. The sky was clear again, the sun shining down and starting to melt the snow. Then, like the night before, it fell from the sky like a flaming meteor, disappearing below the horizon, sizzling as it sank into the snow. The thick darkness of night surrounded their tent.

As Nikki lay down to sleep, utterly exhausted, she wondered where Naomi, Slobber and Peter were. Even though Naomi had been plenty mean plenty of times, she still hoped they were all okay.

15

Whack-a-Weeble

For Naomi, yesterday had been an annoying day for a lot of reasons. First there was the Weeble rodeo, which was awesome. But then came the freezing cold morning and Nikki and Mike both moving up in the Power Rankings for basically doing *nothing* except making a fire and roasting some marshmallows. *How dumb is that?* Then she finally went off with only her sidekick, but Peter had to go and ruin it by following them. As they traipsed through the snow toward a big gray mountain, Peter wouldn't shut up. First he started coming up with words that rhymed with snow. *Crow, dough, go, mow, flow.* Eventually, Naomi had come up with her own word that rhymed. "NO!" she had shouted. "No more rhyming with snow." Of course, that's when Peter began rhyming with "ice." *Nice, mice, slice, rice, dice.* It was only when she hit him in the chest with an ice ball that he finally stopped. Next came the Christmas songs. Apparently snow always made Peter think of Christmas, which was his favorite holiday. To make things worse, Slobber loved Christmas too, and merrily joined in the singing. After the hundredth round of *Jingle Bells*, Naomi was still trying to decide who had the worst voice.

Grrrr. Even thinking about it when she woke up today made Naomi's blood turn to fire. She wanted to push Peter in the snow and bury him. Maybe hundreds of years from now great explorers would find him, thaw him out, and show him their flying cars and time machines.

Slobber, at least, would listen and obey. Naomi knew it was because he was a little scared of her. Maybe a lot scared of her. But Peter…he was missing too many brain cells to be scared of anything. If there was a dragon lying in front of them with its mouth open, she knew Peter would walk right inside thinking it was a warm cave.

The only good thing about yesterday, however, was that nothing tried to fall on them. No giant raindrops, no enormous onion rings, no nothing. It was pretty boring, but sometimes boring was good, right?

But then Naomi rubbed the sleep out of her eyes and blinked. They'd had no choice but to sleep nestled together in the snow under the shelter of a large pine tree. Above her the pine needles had formed into strange patterns that looked like numbers and words. She blinked again, and realized they *were* numbers and words. The Power Rankings! While she and her two bumbling partners had a very uneventful day on the Power Island, something big must've happened to the rest of the power kids and their sidekicks. Britney, of all people, was #1! And to make matters worse, there were now three kids in front of Naomi, including her biggest rival, Nikki Powergloves.

She groaned and rolled over to find Peter Powerhats staring at her, far too close for comfort. "Beep boop beeeeooooop!" he said. She screwed up her face, wishing once more that she'd buried him in the snow. "That's robot for 'Good morning,'" Peter explained.

"Fascinating," Naomi said, rolling over to the other side. She cringed. Slobber was still sleeping, pressed right up against her, a line of drool streaming from his lip to his chin to his arm. The river of slobber had flowed down Slobber's arm and sunk into Naomi's clothes. "Blech!" she cried, standing up so quickly it awakened her sidekick.

"I don't want to go to shchool today, Mommy," Slobber muttered, yawning and wiping the drool from his mouth. His lips were crusted with dried white spittle. *Gross.*

"I ain't your mommy," Naomi said. "And don't worry, today will be much more fun than school. Today is the day we find that pesky Power Giver and *I* win the ultimate prize."

Naomi looked around. Her eyes widened and she blinked a few more times to make sure she wasn't seeing things. The snow was gone. The ice was gone. The sky was blue and lined with long golden clouds. Everything was made of stone. Well, everything except the lone pine tree they had slept under. All of the other trees and bushes stood like statues, carved from hard black rock.

Naomi realized her back was aching. Even the ground was hard and rocky! Wind was rushing across the barren landscape, whipping through her hair. *At least it's not cold*, she thought. If anything, it was slightly warm. Not as hot as two days earlier, when they'd started on the beach, but warm enough to be comfortable. She began peeling off the layers of weird undie-clothing, tossing them on the rocky ground. Nearby, her partners were doing the same, while Peter attempted to teach Slobber "robot language."

"Beepity beep beep BEEP!" Peter said.

"Uh, Beepy boop bope?" Slobber responded.

Peter laughed. "You just called me a poo brain." Slobber laughed too.

Naomi shook her head. At least they were getting along. If Sue were here, they'd all be trying to fight each other. "Let's go," she said. "In less than a day we'll all turn ten years old, and we need to find the Power Giver before that happens."

"Why?" Peter asked.

Had he not listened to anything George Powerglasses said? "Because if we don't, our powers will disappear forever," Naomi explained.

"Why?" Peter asked.

"Because George Powerglasses said so."

"Why?"

"Because the Power Giver told him to."

"Why?"

"You'll have to ask the Power Giver."

"Why?"

This is going to be a long day, Naomi thought.

She did her best to ignore Peter and Slobber as they started rhyming with "rock," and headed toward the gray mountain she'd seen the day before. Of course, without Seth as their guide, she was only guessing where to go. But somehow she knew that the mountain was *exactly* where they needed to go.

"Clock," Peter said.

"Talk," Slobber said.

"Block."

"Flock."

Hawk, mock, dock, knock, jock, sock, walk, Naomi rattled off in her head.

"Box," Peter said.

Naomi stopped walking. "That doesn't rhyme with rock," she said.

Peter nodded. "I know. Technically 'box' is the plural. But the singular does rhyme with rock."

"Box *is* the singular," Naomi said.

"No, it's not," Peter said. "Bock is the singular, as in *go get me that bock!* The plural is box, as in *go get me that box!*"

Naomi knew she couldn't argue with Peter, who clearly had rocks for brains. "Carry on," she said, starting to walk again, more quickly this time. Soon Peter and Slobber were back to rhyming, but with box instead of rock.

"Fox."

"Blocksh."

"Socks."

Naomi had the urge to kick Peter in the shins, but settled for a rock, watching it skitter across the stony ground. With each step it seemed to get a little hotter, as if they were marching into an enormous oven. Also, the terrain began to rise. They'd reached the foothills of the gray mountain, which rose high above them into the golden clouds. *That's where we're going*, Naomi thought.

She felt an ache in her stomach. *Hunger.* They hadn't eaten since Mike created all that food. Maybe she'd been a little harsh about his food power. She certainly wished she had him here now. He could make bacon and eggs, or pancakes with maple syrup, or anything else she wanted. *Mmmm*, she thought, almost able to taste breakfast on her tongue.

To distract herself from Peter and Slobber, who were now singing *She'll Be Coming Round the Mountain*, and her growing hunger, Naomi continued kicking rocks, trying to make each one go a little farther than the last. She gave one a big kick and it bounced, skidded, and then disappeared.

"Huh?" Naomi said to herself. *There must be a hole or something.*

But then the stone popped back up and bounced down the mountain toward her. She stopped, and it settled at her feet, spinning like a top. "Weird," she said.

"She'll be ridin' six wide horses when she cooooomes!" Peter sang.

"Shut up for a sec," Naomi said.

Peter shut up. Slobber drooled. They all stared at the spinning stone, which slowed and then stopped. Peter bent down and picked it up, and then threw it. As when Naomi had kicked it, the rock bounced, skidded, and vanished. "Cool!" Peter said. "Cool, fool, pool—"

"Drool," Slobber added.

The rock popped from wherever it had disappeared to. Gravity took over and it clanked and rattled down the mountainside, bouncing past them and back the way they'd come.

"Nishe trick," Slobber said.

"It's no trick," Naomi said, frowning. "Something is there. It could be a trap."

Just as she said the word 'trap,' a furry green head popped out from the rock. "Na na-na na-na naaaaa!" the Weeble taunted, sticking its thumbs in its ears. "You can't whack me!"

Naomi's hand suddenly felt heavier than before, and she looked down to find a big wooden mallet grasped in her fingers.

"Are we playing crochet?" Peter asked. He also had a big hammer. Slobber wasn't left out of the fun either.

Naomi smiled. "No," she said. "We're playing Whack-a-Weeble."

While Peter and Slobber discussed what she meant by that, Naomi quickly changed into her orange skirt and raced up the mountainside. The green Weeble had disappeared into his hole, but another one—pink with white spots—had appeared a little further up. The nasty little creature stuck its tongue out at her and made a farting noise. Then it disappeared.

Naomi gritted her teeth and scanned the mountain, which was dotted with black holes. She could feel the heat of lasers building up in her eyes. All she had to do was wink at the next Weeble she saw.

"Boo!" a voice shouted behind her. Naomi practically jumped out of her skin but managed to spin around, simultaneously winking a few lasers at a neon blue Weeble that was already disappearing back into its hole. "So long, sucker!" the Weeble yelled as the lasers shot harmlessly over its head.

Slobber had caught up, and was now swinging his mallet at anything that moved, as Weebles began popping up all over the place. They were all different colors, and each of them had a different taunt ready. "My grandma is faster than you!" "Can't catch me, slowpoke!" and "You swing like a normal kid!" were some of their favorites.

Peter, who was wearing his neon-green hat, had grown big and strong, and was slamming his hammer like a lumberjack splitting wood. He completely missed one Weeble, almost caught the next before it disappeared back into its hole, and whacked the third one right on the noggin. The Weeble wobbled back and forth, said, "Hooray for you," and then fell back into its hole.

"Hooray for me!" Peter agreed.

A big smooth stone block appeared nearby, and names and rankings were chiseled into it. They were unchanged from before, except for #7, where Peter had replaced Tanya.

Naomi licked her lips. Peter had only whacked one Weeble, and already he was in the top 7! She knew this was her chance to get back into first place. All she had to do was catch these silly Weebles.

She refocused on the task, spinning and running and leaping and shooting lasers in every direction. One Weeble got hit by her laser and it was so stunned that she managed to whack it with her mallet. Another dodged a laser, but she was still able to smack it upside the head. Each Weeble that got hit fell into its hole and didn't pop out again. Peter managed to whack at least three, while she nailed so many she lost count. Slobber managed just one, but Naomi didn't really care.

By the time the Weebles stopped popping their heads from the holes, the Power Rankings were looking much better to Naomi:

1. Naomi Powerskirts
2. Britney Powerearrings
3. Nikki Powergloves
4. Samantha Powerbelts
5. Peter Powerhats
6. Sue Powerslippers
7. Mike Powerscarves
8. Tanya Powershirts

"Yes!" Naomi said, raising her hammer over her head. She winked a bunch of lasers into the air, watching them whizz through the sky like fireworks. She'd done it. She was back in first. Now she just had to find the Power Giver before the day was over.

"Five five five!" Peter crowed, doing a dance and flexing his ginormous muscles.

"Alive alive alive!" Slobber joined in, whirling in a circle, flinging drool in every direction.

Even though they looked ridiculous, Naomi was strangely happy to have the two big oafs to share this moment with. "Good job," she said. "But we're not done yet."

They started back up the mountain, which was getting steeper with every step. It was also getting hotter. Naomi felt beads of sweat rolling down her cheeks, and used her shirt to wipe them away. Less than ten seconds later, more sweat was dripping from her chin. It was like they were being cooked alive. In this heat, there was no way they'd make it to the top of the mountain!

Luckily, they didn't have to. When they were about halfway to the golden clouds that ringed the peak, they came upon a dark cave. Naomi remembered her thought from earlier, about how Peter would probably walk into a dragon's mouth thinking it was a cave. She hoped she wasn't about to make that same mistake.

But going through the mountain seemed like a much better option than going over or around.

"I'm not going in there," Slobber said.

"Suit yourself," Naomi said. "You can stay here *all alone*." She knew it was a mean thing to say to her sidekick, but she didn't really mean it. She wouldn't really leave him behind. It was just a trick to get him to come. And it worked.

"No, no, no, I'll come, I'll come," Slobber said, following her into the dark.

Peter switched to his orange hat and began burping fireballs to light the way. Naomi contributed too, winking lasers ahead of them. Slobber tried to cling to her arm, but she pushed him away. *Big sissy!* she thought.

Like on the mountain, it seemed to get hotter with each step, until she had to tell Peter to stop burping fireballs.

The tunnel was dark, but not too long, and soon Naomi could see a circle of light ahead. "There!" she said. "Hurry, we're close now."

The three kids rushed forward to the end, with Naomi in the lead. As the tunnel ended, Naomi's eyes widened and she skidded to a stop, nearly tumbling over the edge of a cliff that fell so far she couldn't see the bottom. Unfortunately, she had two big boys behind her, each of whom crashed into her. First Slobber bumped her, and then Peter bumped Slobber.

Fear stole Naomi's breath as she lost her footing and fell over the side. Slobber and Peter both reached for her, but her sweaty fingers slipped away, unable to grab them. Empty air swallowed her, pushing her heart into her throat.

This is it. This is the end, she thought.

But then something grabbed her around the ankles and she stopped falling, bouncing once and then swinging wildly, colliding with the cliff wall. "Ouch!" she said.

She was upside down, still swinging in the wind. Below her was empty space. She didn't want to look down, so she looked up to find two long green vines wrapped around each of her ankles. Slowly, slowly, the vines were pulling her back up the cliff.

When she neared the top, Peter and Slobber grabbed hold and hoisted Naomi onto her feet. Her heart was pounding and it was hard to breathe. "Oh my gosh, oh my gosh, oh my gosh," she panted.

She watched as the vines slithered away from her, coasting along a thin shelf of rock running along the cliff's edge. She followed their path until they reached a pair of familiar shoes. Her gaze travelled upwards to a girl wearing green gloves.

Once more, she lost her breath.

Nikki Powergloves had saved her life.

16

To the rest of you...good luck!

Before Nikki and the Power Team had begun their march up the gray mountain, Mike had taken breakfast orders, leaving Nikki's stomach full of her favorite cereal, Chocolate-Covered Sugar Wheats. As Spencer liked to joke, it was good brain food. After breakfast, they'd stripped off all their undie-clothing because they didn't seem to need it anymore.

Nothing had happened as they climbed the mountain, which, in Nikki's opinion, was a good thing. She just wanted to get to the Power Giver before someone got crushed by a giant onion or confused by some weird place where everything was the opposite of what you expected.

She didn't even mind the new rocky terrain or how hot it was getting. It was better than the cold snow and ice from the day before!

When they'd reached a dusty old path that went around the mountain, Samantha said they should vote on whether to follow it. Sue thought *she* should make the decision herself, but eventually agreed to a vote and the majority decided to take the path anyway. Everyone was surprisingly happy, even when the path got narrower and narrower.

That's when she'd heard an unexpected sound. A voice had echoed from somewhere in front of them, and she'd heard the scuff of running feet. Before Nikki knew what was happening, Naomi had emerged from a cave and tumbled over the cliff's edge.

And Nikki had saved her. She didn't really think about the fact that it was Naomi she was saving, the girl who'd abandoned them. She just knew it was a kid who needed her help, so she used her green gloves to grow vines.

"Nikki," Naomi said now, her eyes as wide as flying saucers.

"Naomi," Nikki said.

"Why did you…but you didn't have to…if you hadn't done that…" For once, Naomi was at a loss for words. She was just a scared girl who needed help.

"Everyone needs a little help sometimes," Nikki said.

"Not me," Naomi said. "Not until now. I always win on my own."

"Things change," Nikki said. "People change."

"Not me," Naomi said again, but this time she sounded less sure of herself.

"It's okay," Nikki said. "You don't always have to be so tough all the time."

It was the wrong thing to say. Naomi's eyes narrowed and she frowned. "I am tough," she said. "Tougher than you. Tougher than your friends. Tougher than everybody. And don't think what happened is going to make any difference. I'm not going to let you win."

"What a jerk," Samantha whispered from behind Nikki.

Nikki nodded, but in her heart she wasn't so sure that any of them really knew who Naomi was on the inside, behind her prickly wall of meanness.

Before she could think any more about it, however, there was a burst of heat from deep below. All the kids looked down to find a thick, oozing, bubbling liquid rising toward them, filling the canyon.

"Lava!" Spencer exclaimed. No wonder it was getting hotter and hotter.

They had nowhere to go, nowhere to run. If the lava rose much higher, it would cover them all. Nikki looked at Seth, to see if he was worried, but he had a big smile on his face. "What?" Nikki said. "Why are you smiling?"

"Because our quest is almost over," Seth said. "Good enough!" he shouted, and the lava stopped rising. Big bubbles grew and popped, superheated by the fiery flow.

"What's on the other side?" Freddy asked, peering into the distance. Nikki looked, too. She thought she could see another mountain, but the fog was so thick she wasn't sure.

"Your destiny!" a voice shouted from above. Nikki looked up to see a flaming torch of a boy, his red eyes gleaming.

"George?" Spencer said. "Is that you?"

George the red-eyed human fireball smiled a fiery smile. He was wearing bright red glasses ringed with fire. "The Power Island is split into two sides, separated by this chasm of lava. You can choose to stay on this side, or attempt to cross."

"I'm crossing," Naomi said, her arms folded over her chest.

"But beware," George continued as if she hadn't spoken, "your flying powers are useless here." He looked up at the golden clouds.

Naomi blew out a huff of air. "I'm still crossing," she said.

"Good," George said. "I hope you all choose to cross."

The rest of the kids looked around at each other. "I will," Nikki said. The others nodded in agreement.

Sue pushed forward to the front, next to Nikki. "What do we get if we make it across?" she asked.

"A chance," George said.

"A chance for what?" Freddy asked.

"A chance," George repeated. "Now, down to business. You have two options for crossing. On your own, using one of these…" From his fist, he shot a fireball into the thick, oozing lava below. There was an explosion of heat and a burst of steam, which stung Nikki's eyes. She blinked away the tears, and when her vision cleared she found three new paths across the lava.

The first was a bridge, or at least that's the only word she could think of to call it. But as far as bridges go, it wasn't too impressive. Built with rickety old wooden boards, the bridge looked on the verge of collapsing into the lava at any moment. Old rusty nails protruded from the sides at strange, disjointed angles. Fire seemed to be slowly creeping up the concrete pillars that held the bridge aloft.

The second option was a rope. Strung from the rock above them, it looked threadbare and worn, as if it might snap at any second. It hung loosely over the lava, sagging in the middle. Something was crawling along it. *Spiders*, Nikki realized. Not little spiders, but hairy tarantulas with long legs that made Nikki's skin crawl.

The third and final crossing was a series of rock platforms rising up from the lava. The first few were fairly large and close together, and Nikki thought it would be easy to jump from one to the next, but the further into the canyon you got, the platforms became smaller and further apart.

All three crossings disappeared into a thick mist, so Nikki couldn't see where they ended. On the other side, she hoped.

"You said there were two options," Samantha said, "but there are three crossings."

George said, "The three crossings are one option. If you choose them, you will have the chance to greatly improve in the Power Rankings."

"And if we choose not to use the three crossings?" Axel said.

"Your Power Ranking cannot go up," George said.

Nikki frowned. "Why would anyone choose that option?" she asked.

"Because it's much safer, my lady," Seth announced. "The second option will be me, and I promise to get you safely across to the other side. Well, me and my undie slingshot."

"But if we choose that option we can't move up in the Power Rankings?" Mike clarified.

"Correct," George said. "At least not in this challenge. But you may still move up in future challenges."

Nikki considered the options. "I think you should take the slingshot," she said to Spencer. "I'll try the crossings."

Spencer hummed softly to himself. Other kids were discussing the options with each other and their sidekicks too. Finally, Spencer said, "I think we should both use Seth's slingshot. The three crossings are too dangerous."

Although Spencer's suggestion was smart, she wasn't Nikki Nickerson anymore. She was Nikki Powergloves, a superhero, and she couldn't run from danger ever again. She had to be brave. "I have to do this, Spence," she said.

He nodded. "I know. And as your sidekick, I have to help you."

Nikki shook her head rapidly. "No you don't, Spence. You've already done so much to help me. Take the slingshot and I'll see you on the other side."

But from the determined look in Spencer's eyes, Nikki knew her friend wasn't going to budge. "I'm coming," he said.

Nikki put an arm around him. "Thank you." It was the only thing she could say.

The rest of the Power Team had also made their decisions, separating into two groups. On one side was Naomi, who was clearly going to try the crossings. Nikki admired her courage, especially after she'd almost fallen into the canyon once already. Around her were Axel and June, Samantha and Dexter, Tyrone and Weasel, Mike, and Tanya. Standing toward the back was one other power kid: Britney. Nikki was surprised to see her there, not because she didn't think Britney was good or strong enough, but because Britney had always struggled with self-confidence. Nikki and Spencer moved over to the group that was taking the crossings. Samantha grinned at them and Mike gave them high-fives.

"You can do this," Nikki said to Britney.

Britney smiled at her. "I know," she said. "For the first time in my life, I know I'm ready for something."

Warmth swelled in Nikki's heart. This was what being a superhero was all about. Trusting yourself to be able to do things no one else could do.

She turned to look at those in the other group. At the front was Sue, who was wearing a smug grin, like she knew something none of the rest of them knew. On either side of her were Sharkey and Slobber. Behind her were Freddy, Peter, Jimmy and Tanya.

"Sorry, guys," Freddy said. "This is too much." He pointed at the lava. "Be safe and I'll see you on the other side."

Seth said, "You're up, Freddy!" and pulled back a giant undie slingshot that appeared from thin air. Freddy eased back into the white cocoon and grinned at the rest of them.

Samantha said, "See you soon," and Seth released the slingshot, which shot forward with a *thwump!*

"AHHHHHhhhhhhhhhhhhhhhhhhhhhhhhhh!" Freddy cried, his voice getting softer and softer as he flew further and further away, vanishing into the mist.

"Um," Sharkey said. "Are you sure he made it?"

"Of course!" Seth said. "I'm at least fifty percent sure."

"But that's like flipping a coin," Sharkey said.

Seth grinned. "Yep. Your turn!" Sharkey seemed like she might make a run for it, but Sue pushed her into the slingshot. "Hey!" Sharkey cried.

But it was far too late to change her mind. The slingshot twanged and then Sharkey was gone, following Freddy into the mist.

Peter, Jimmy and Tanya followed soon after. Jimmy flew straight and fast, like a torpedo—he was used to flying with his rocket boots. Peter was less graceful, his arms and legs flying all around his thick body. Tanya held out her arms like an airplane soaring through the air.

Sue was next. She offered a sugar-sweet smile. "See you at your funerals," she said. And then she was gone too.

Last was Slobber, who looked the most uneasy of the bunch. "Last chance to switch sides," Naomi said. "You do this and you'll have to find yourself a superhero who wants a chicken for a sidekick."

Nikki gasped. *Naomi was getting rid of her sidekick if he didn't choose the dangerous crossings?* She wanted to speak up, to say something, but there was nothing she could say. She already had a sidekick.

"I—I'm sorry," Slobber said. A moment later, Seth shot him over the lava and into the mist.

"What a wimp," Naomi muttered. "I don't need him anyway." She turned away, but Nikki thought she saw a tear in her eye before Naomi could hide it.

Seth was the last to go. "Can someone pull me?" he asked as he sat in the giant underwear slingshot.

"Sure, small-fry," Tyrone said, sauntering over. With one big hand, he stretched the slingshot so far back Nikki thought it might break.

Seth looked over and said, "Four power kids and two sidekicks are safe and sound. To the rest of you…good luck!" Tyrone released the slingshot and Seth disappeared from view.

Spencer leaned over to say something to Nikki, but just then there was an explosion of laughter from above them. The remaining kids looked up to find hundreds of Weebles perched on the mountain, giggling and chuckling and laughing.

Nikki took a deep breath. She knew from experience why the Weebles were here.

The Weebles were here for the show.

17

Lava, Weebles, and George Powerglasses

Even though there were only three crossings to choose from, Nikki couldn't decide. Spencer couldn't either. "The rope," he said. "No, wait, maybe the rock platforms. Or the bridge. Yeah, the bridge!"

Nikki had never seen Spencer so confused. Perhaps it was because all three crossings looked like awful choices. She wondered whether Seth's slingshot might've been the smart move after all.

The other kids were having less trouble. Naomi was already wearing her gray skirt and balancing on the rope like a tightrope. The tarantulas scurried toward her, but she simply hopped over them. Samantha had on her yellow "spider" belt, and was crawling underneath the rope with Dexter hanging onto her back. Any time a tarantula got too close, Dexter would spray it with a poof of brown gas from a canister.

"What is that stuff?" Nikki asked.

"One of Dexter's inventions," Spencer said. "Stink gas. Keeps away friends, foes, and tarantulas."

The brown gas rose up around Naomi as she balanced on the rope. "Yuck!" she screamed, almost falling. "Someone stinks!"

While Naomi was trying not to lose her balance, Samantha and Dexter raced ahead of her.

Nikki glanced over at the crossing with the rock platforms. Mike had his blue-and-gold striped scarf wrapped around his neck. In his hands was a long pole. He ran along the cliff and then stuck the pole into the ground. It bent, but didn't break, and propelled him into the air. He flew from the cliff onto the first platform, landing lightly on the balls of his feet. He was off to a great start. As Mike pole-vaulted to the next platform, Britney jumped onto the first. Just before she landed, a lush bed of flowers appeared, cushioning her fall.

The rickety bridge already had kids on it, too. Axel was wearing a green pullover jacket and had shrunk down to elf size. He even had pointy ears! He was running along the bridge just in front of June. The bridge creaked and swayed, but anytime he or June started to lose their balance he would shoot off a rainbow from his fingertips. The tiny rainbows were solid, and the kids were able to grab them to keep themselves steady. Tyrone was also on the bridge, wearing a black belt with a big gold buckle. He was riding a beautiful gold mustang, with Weasel hanging on behind him. The stallion galloped across the bridge so fast that even when the boards cracked under its hooves they didn't fall through.

All the kids were doing really well—at least, until the lava, Weebles, and George Powerglasses got involved. Huge bursts of lava erupted from below. It sprayed around Samantha, Dexter, and Naomi on the rope. They screamed as they did their best to avoid the fiery blobs of molten rock. The Weebles started throwing things—tomatoes, eggs, pickles...Nikki even saw a particularly large blue Weeble chuck a frozen dinner like a Frisbee. The food rained down on Mike and Britney on the rock platforms. An egg hit Mike in the nose, and he fell, grabbing the edge at the last moment. As he pulled himself up, yoke dripped down his chin. Britney hid in one of her flowerbeds as a dozen tomatoes splatted around her. George, who had never attacked any of them before, began shooting flaming lasers from his eyes. The lasers scorched the bridge, setting the handrail on fire, and sending Tyrone's horse running back the way it had come. Elf Axel and June were forced to stop and use rainbows to put out the fires one by one.

As Nikki watched all the other kids struggling, she became even more confused as to which path to take.

Then something dawned on her. "Spence, why can't we take all three?"

Spencer looked at her and raised an eyebrow. "What do you—hey! That's a great idea!"

Nikki nodded. It was the only way. "We'll take whichever path is the easiest at first, and then switch to the next easiest one," she said.

Spencer grinned and nodded. "Which one first?"

At the same time, they both said, "Rocky platforms." Even though the Weebles were throwing food at Britney and Mike, the platforms were wide and safe, and Nikki would rather face a food fight than lava or George's fire lasers.

Nikki also knew exactly which powers to use. "Ice and speed!" she yelled, slipping on one white and one orange glove.

"Go!" Spencer shouted, and they took off toward the platforms.

Just before they reached the gap between the cliff and the first platform, Nikki yelled, "Slide!" and shot ice from her fingertips. The ice formed a bridge through the air. She slid feet first, spraying cold wet ice around her. Behind her, Spencer dove headfirst. On the first platform, they collided with one of Britney's flowerbeds, which was covered in red tomato slime.

"Good start," Spencer said, as more food flew over their heads. "And now it's time for my latest invention—pocket paddle!"

"Huh?" Nikki said.

Spencer reached into his pocket and withdrew a strange white wand. He blew into one end and a big paddle popped from the other end. It looked like a ping-pong paddle, only much bigger. It was even bigger than Spencer's head. When the next tomato flew toward them, Spencer swung the paddle, smashing the fruit before it could hit them. Something heavier arced through the air—a potato—and when Spencer whacked it, the potato deflected back toward the mountain, bouncing off the Weeble who threw it in the first place. "Ouch!" the Weeble cried. "Ow ow ow ow ow!!!"

"Serves you right!" Spencer responded.

From there, they slid on Nikki's ice bridges from platform to platform, while Spencer used his pocket paddle to knock flying food out of the air.

When they passed Britney, Nikki said, "You can do it!"

"Thanks," Britney said, dodging a flying pizza.

When they passed Mike, Spencer said, "Keep going, you'll make it!"

Mike said, "You too!" and used his pole to fend off an entire watermelon heading for him.

When the mist swirled around them and the platforms got too small for them both to fit on, Nikki said, "Time to switch crossings!" She shot an ice bridge from the platforms over to the old wooden bridge and they slid across, grabbing the wooden railing to hang on. They wood cracked, but didn't break. Tyrone, Weasel, and the mustang were behind them. Tyrone and his sidekick had dismounted and were trying to stamp out the fires and calm down the horse, which was reared up on two legs. Despite their efforts, the boards were splintering beneath their weight. Any second they could fall through and into the lava.

Nikki aimed six or seven ice pellets at the fire, and soon the flames were doused. "Thanks!" Tyrone and Weasel said at the same time. They leapt onto the mustang and resumed their gallop across the bridge.

Nikki and Spencer ran, chasing after Axel and June, who were slowly crossing the bridge, using rainbows to block George's fire lasers. As they caught up, George noticed them. "Sorry about this, Power Giver's orders!" he said, shooting lasers from his eyes.

"I'm sorry, too," Nikki said, blocking the lasers with an ice shield. Then she fired a powerful burst of ice at George. He tried to dodge it, but the ice clipped his toes. As the ice crept up his legs to his stomach and chest, the fire all around his body went out, sending plumes of steam into the air.

"Well done, Nikki," George said, just before the ice froze his mouth closed and his eyes shut. He dropped from the sky, and for a moment Nikki was scared that he'd sink into the lava. But then he vanished with a blinding burst of light.

"Yeah!" Tyrone, Weasel, Axel, June, and Spencer yelled. Spencer was the loudest of all.

They continued along the bridge, which seemed to get weaker and more broken with each step. Soon it was missing boards, parts of the handrail, and even entire sections. Mike and Britney had followed Nikki's lead and left the rocky platforms for the bridge. The kids huddled together to discuss the problem.

"We have to switch to the rope," Nikki said.

"I don't know if I can do it," Mike said, clutching at his scarf.

Nikki was about to say something, but Britney beat her to it. "Yes, you can," she said. "I've looked up to you and the others for a long time. You are an incredible superhero."

Mike seemed startled by the compliment. "I, uh, thank you," he said. He took a deep breath. "You're right. I can do this."

Nikki was so proud of her friends. Britney had found her courage and Mike was braver than he even knew. "Follow me," Nikki said, creating an ice bridge over to the rope.

Together, the power kids and sidekicks slid across, trying not to look down into the molten rock below. They grabbed the rope, hanging on for dear life. Samantha and Dexter were nearby, still trying to dodge the tarantulas and bursts of lava. Naomi was ahead, dancing across the rope like it was a strong, thick bridge.

"Stay together!" Nikki said. "We have to do this as a team!"

Naomi only laughed and ran further ahead.

Nikki gritted her teeth and focused on the rest of the kids. Mike was hanging on with one hand and using his other hand to poke the tarantulas with his pole. Britney was dropping flowerbeds on the spouts of lava, smothering them. Tyrone's horse had disappeared and he was using all of his strength to hang onto Weasel. Axel was creating rainbow hoops around the rope. Weasel grabbed one and it immediately began to slide along the rope like a zip line. "Woohoo!" she yelled.

Axel slid a rainbow hoop to each of the other kids. "Hang on tight, don't look down, and have fun," he said. One by one, the kids slid along the rope, until only Nikki and Axel remained. "Your turn," Axel said.

Nikki grinned. "You know you have real friends now, right?" she said.

Axel nodded. "Yes. I'm not scared of losing the Power Team anymore. June taught me that."

"Good," Nikki said. "She's a good sidekick. See you on the other side!" With that, she grabbed the rainbow, which was warm to the touch, and bent her knees. As the rope sagged under her weight, she gained speed, whizzing past the lava, which bubbled and steamed below her. "Yeah!" she exclaimed, loving the feel of the wind through her hair. It was almost as good as flying.

The rope went on and on and on, and she still couldn't see the other side of the canyon. Her fingers were getting tired and sweaty, and were slipping from the rainbow hoop. *Hang on*, she thought. *Just hang on a little longer.* The mist was getting thinner and she could see farther ahead.

A wide rocky cliff appeared first, and then her friends. They were all there, both the kids that took Seth's slingshot, and the rest of them.

But her fingers were so tired. And so slippery. "Hang on, hang on, hang on," she muttered to herself, even as one hand slipped from the rainbow. Her body jerked as she clutched at the hoop with only one hand. Another finger popped off, then another. She was clinging to the rainbow with only two fingers and a thumb.

She was so close. So very close. She wanted to shoot an ice bridge, but was afraid it would only throw off her concentration. As her last three fingers slipped from the rainbow, she saw a shadow above her, dancing along the rope.

Her body twisted in midair and all she saw was red. Lava, fiery hot and molten, writhed like an angry ocean beneath her. This was it. She was falling and couldn't do anything to save herself.

Her body jerked as something clamped onto her collar. "Gotcha!" a familiar voice cried. A strong arm pulled her up onto the rope.

When she saw who it was, her eyes widened in surprise. "Naomi?" she said.

"Nikki," Naomi said, her eyes dark with amusement. "This is for saving me. Now we're even."

Nikki didn't know what to say, except, "Thank you," but Naomi was already gone, running along the rope and jumping onto the other side of the island.

18

Goodbye friends

Naomi didn't know why she'd saved Nikki Powergloves. She told herself it was just because Nikki had saved her, but she knew she was lying to herself. In that moment, she'd seen someone who needed help, and so she'd helped her. It was that simple.

Naomi shook her head to clear the cobwebs. She'd felt so many different emotions in the last couple of days that she didn't know what to think anymore. Anger, sadness, surprise, thankfulness, and yeah, even a little fear. She almost felt like she was a different girl in the same skin. It was a weird feeling.

The other kids were gathered around Nikki, making sure she was okay. Axel had made it safely across, too, and Naomi felt relieved about that although she didn't know why she should care about Axel.

No one came over to Naomi for a while, but then, slowly, they did. "Thanks for saving Nikki," Samantha said. The others were crowded around behind her. A few of them murmured "Good job" and "Thank you" but Naomi wasn't interested in hearing that.

"What are the new Power Rankings?" she said to the sky.

"Is that why you did it?" Samantha asked. "Just to move up in the Power Rankings?"

"Yes," Naomi answered automatically, even though she knew it wasn't true.

"Behold! The Power Rankings!" Seth said, pointing to the sky.

The swirls of mist swirled and misted, forming letters and numbers and names.

1. Naomi Powerskirts
2. Axel Powerjackets
3. Nikki Powergloves
4. Britney Powerearrings
5. Samantha Powerbelts
6. Mike Powerscarves
7. Tyrone Powerbling
8. Sue Powerslippers
9. Tanya Powershirts

For the first time, Naomi didn't feel anything when she saw her name in first place. She didn't feel happy or sad or excited or thrilled. Just…nothing. She forced herself to smile and clap her hands, but it wasn't real. It was just an act.

"Eighth place!?" Sue complained. "I'm better than all seven of the kids in front of me."

"Actually, you're not," George Powerglasses said, stepping from behind a rock. He was wearing dark black sunglasses, which he pushed down his nose so he could look at them. "And I did warn you that taking the easy route across the gorge would hurt you in the rankings."

"The easy way?" Sue shrieked. "Is that what you call it? Does this *look* easy?" She pointed to her elbows and knees, which were scraped and bleeding. Naomi hadn't noticed before, but now that she looked closer, all the kids who had used Seth's slingshot were cut, bruised, or scraped. She felt a little bad for them. *What is wrong with me?* she wondered. *They're LOSERS, little twerps to be stepped over so I can win the ultimate prize.* But in her heart, she knew they were more than that, even if she wasn't ready to admit it.

Seth pulled his underwear up a little further. "I was in charge of the flight, not the landing."

"You little punk..." Sue growled. She stalked toward him, her fists raised. But when she tried to hit him, her fist went...well, it went right *through* him.

Naomi gawked. A hole had appeared in Seth's shoulder. Sue's eyes widened as she pulled her fist out. The hole disappeared as if it had never been there in the first place. She swung again, this time aiming for Seth's stomach, but, once again, her fist went in one side of UnderMan and out the other. There was a hole in his stomach.

Sue withdrew her hand and took a step back.

"Hee hee, you can't hit mee!" Seth sang. "You can't hit mee, 'cause I'm made of Swiss cheeeeese!"

"Whatever," Sue said. "Let's just get on with it. What's the next challenge? I'm going to win it."

"You'll see," George said. He dropped to all fours, his body darkening as black fur covered him. His hands and feet turned to paws and his fingernails to claws. His teeth became fangs. He let out a real growl that put Sue's growl to shame, and then took off.

"That dude is strange," Tyrone said. "But I kind of like him."

Me too, Naomi almost blurted out. Instead she just said, "I'm going after him," and started running.

"Wait, hold on a second," Nikki said.

Naomi stopped. She turned. "What?" she said, her hands on her hips. She didn't have time for this. She was trying to win.

"We should stick together as a team," Nikki said.

"Ha!" Naomi laughed. "We're not a team."

"But back at the Power City you said you'd join the Power Team so you could come on this adventure." Nikki was frowning, and for some reason it made Naomi feel sort of sad on the inside.

But on the outside she was all hard edges. "Newsflash, Nikki, *I lied.* I only told you all what you wanted to hear so I could come. But I'm not here for you, or George, or anyone else. I'm here for *myself.*" Nikki's face went all red, which would normally make Naomi laugh, but not this time. This time she felt a knot form in her gut. *Why am I being so mean?* she asked herself. *Is this really who I am?* It was like she couldn't help herself. "C'mon, Slobber," she said. "We don't need these fools."

A surprised look crossed Slobber's face. He had a few cuts on his cheeks and one of his eyes was black. He must've landed really hard. "But you shaid if I took Sheth's shlingshot I wouldn't be your shidekick anymore."

"I was just overreacting," Naomi said. "I was just trying to get you to come with me across the rope."

"But I didn't want to come," Slobber said, wiping drool off his chin.

"I know that now," Naomi said. "But you want to come now, right?" Naomi felt herself leaning forward on the balls of her toes. For some reason, his answer felt important to her.

"No," he said, and Naomi's heart sank into the knot in her gut. "I want to be on the Power Team. I thought we were going to be on the Power Team *together.*"

Naomi almost felt like she'd swallowed the lava and it was now running through her entire body. She felt so angry. So incredibly angry, like she could do something crazy. But she knew her anger was just covering up another more powerful emotion.

She turned and walked away. "See you at the finish line, losers," she said, not meaning any of the words.

Inside she only felt sad.

19

Riddled

Naomi was gone, and none of the kids wanted to go after her. Nikki had thought she saw something good in Naomi when they'd each saved each other, but maybe she was mistaken. Naomi was all bad. Bad to the core, like a rotten apple. A villain from top to bottom and side to side.

"You can be my sidekick if you want," Jimmy was saying to Slobber.

"Really?" Slobber said. "I didn't think anyone would want me."

"I've wanted you as my sidekick from the second I saw you throw that football," Jimmy said. Nikki smiled. Jimmy had come a long way from when he'd tried to destroy Cragglyville, and she was happy to call him her friend.

"Yesh," Slobber said. "I'll be your shidekick."

Jimmy smiled the biggest smile Nikki had ever seen. In fact, a lot of the kids were smiling. They'd made it over the lava canyon. After that challenge, they could get past anything.

The only kid not smiling was Sue. "We have to beat that girl," Sue said. "I don't care who wins, as long as it's not Naomi Powerskirts. I want to see her lose! I want to see her crying and—hey! Who threw that?" Nikki didn't know what Sue was talking about, but she was rubbing her cheek. There was a little red spot on her skin, like she'd been hit by something sharp. When no one answered, she said, "Who threw that rock at me?"

All the kids were looking at each other in confusion.

"Ow!" Spencer said, rubbing his head.

"Ouch!" said Freddy, massaging his shoulder.

There were clinks and plinks as tiny pebbles began falling from the sky like rain. One of them stung Nikki's cheek, and another bounced off her arm. They hurt!

"RUN!" Axel yelled.

Kids immediately started changing. Freddy transformed into a turtle as he ran, so the pebbles would bounce off his shell. Axel bulged out and turned orange. Soon he was an actual orange, rolling ahead of everyone. Nikki used her ice power to create an icy shield that she and Spencer held above their heads to protect them while they ran. It was like a hailstorm, only worse. Nikki couldn't help but to worry about Naomi, who was all on her own.

The stony rain got heavier, the rocks bigger. If it got much worse, even their powers wouldn't be able to protect them. A fist-sized rock slammed into Nikki's shield, and it cracked down the middle. She shot some more ice to seal it back together, but then an even bigger rock— about the size of a basketball—smashed into it, crumbling the ice shield around them.

"Ahhh!" Nikki and Spencer yelled together.

The other kids were having just as much trouble. Axel's orange peel had dents and holes in it and was leaking orange juice. Freddy's shell was cracked in at least three places. Britney had become as hard as a diamond, sparkling from head to toe, but even she was struggling as rocks rained down on her head. If they didn't find shelter soon, they'd never make it.

"In here!" Seth yelled to them. He was pointing at a large black cave in the mountainside.

They were so close, and yet still so far away from the cave. Thankfully, Seth was there to help.

His body began to elongate, rolling into a tube with arms and legs and Seth's eyes peeking out. The tube got longer and longer, stretching out to the helpless kids like a huge water pipe. The kids dove inside in bunches, bouncing off each other and falling to the soft underwear floor in groups of three and four.

Above them, bigger and bigger stones bounced off of Seth's pipe-like body. "Holy monkeybites!" Spencer exclaimed, which pretty much summed up the situation. "That was a close one!"

Seth's voice seemed to come from all sides, echoing through the pipe. "Ladies and sirs, if it's not too much trouble, please make your way to the exit and into the cave. These rocks are starting to hurt!"

The kids helped each other up, and then rushed through the dark pipe and into the even darker cave. Someone bumped into Nikki from behind and she bumped into someone else. Kids were shouting and talking all at once, scared and confused.

"Wait!" Nikki said, and everyone quieted down. "Hold on a sec. We need light." She opened her powerchest and rummaged through the gloves, feeling the raised symbols on each until she found the one she wanted. "Fire," she whispered, and a flame appeared on her finger. She concentrated, making it bigger and bigger, until it was like a torch, shining bright enough to light the entire cave.

All at once, everyone gasped, backing up. Behind them, Seth entered the cave, the sound of the rock rainfall muffling his footsteps.

In front of them was something very scary:

An enormous bird, like the ones they saw flying over the forest, stood before them. Its feathers were as black as a moonless night, its beak as long as a sword, and its claws as sharp as shark's teeth. And yet that wasn't the scariest thing about it. What was really freaking Nikki and her friends out was the fact that the bird had three of everything.

Three heads, three beaks, three sets of dark, beady eyes staring at them, three sets of those razor-sharp claws, and three sets of huge wings.

All three beaks began to speak at the same time. "First riddle—second riddle—third riddle," the three beaks said one after another. "My turn!" "No, my turn!" "Me first!" "No, *me* first!"

Nikki realized the three heads were arguing with each other. It would've almost been funny, if not for the fact that each of the three beaks were big enough to swallow her whole.

Seth stepped forward, which Nikki thought was a very brave thing to do. "Ladies," Seth said. "One at a time. Grunhilda first. Then Brunhilda. Then Patsy."

Nikki didn't know what was stranger, that Seth was speaking to the three-headed bird, or that he knew their names.

One of the three opened her mouth. "I am Grunhilda, the most fearsome sister of the Tri-Bird," she said.

The other two birds—Brunhilda and Patsy—interrupted her, cawing and flapping their wings. "Most fearsome? Bah!" one of them said. "You're less fearsome than Cranky the Crab!" the other sister said.

"Ladies!" Seth said. "Please. We don't have time for this. The Power Giver awaits."

"It was *her* fault," one of the sisters said, pointing her beak at Grunhilda.

"Can I help it that I make you jealous, Patsy?" Grunhilda said. That started another round of cawing and wing-flapping. Finally, Seth was able to calm the Tri-Bird down enough for Grunhilda to continue.

"My sincerest apologies for my sisters' behavior," Grunhilda said. "As you may have figured out, we are the Tri-Bird, the keepers of the Cave of Power, where the Power Giver lives. None may enter unless they are pure, true, and wise. Having made it this far, you have already proven yourselves pure and true. But it is yet to be seen whether you are wise. In this challenge, you will be asked three riddles. Answer them correctly and you may pass. Answer them incorrectly and..." The monstrous bird trailed away. Her sisters clacked their beaks together.

Nikki wondered what she meant. Would the birds eat them? She felt goosebumps rise on her neck.

"Oh beautiful and gracious Tri-Bird, what is your first riddle?" Seth asked.

Grunhilda arched her long neck, which made a popping sound. "Ahh," she said. "That's better. The first riddle is this: What sleeps inside and outside, never dreaming, never waking, changing its face from day to night and night to day, always dull and always shining? Speak the answer wise and true, and you shall be rewarded. Speak falsely, and you shall surely..." Again, the bird left the sentence unfinished. The kids' imaginations were sure to make them think the worst.

Nikki tried not to think about what would happen if they couldn't figure out the riddle. Spencer, who had a really good memory, recited the riddle as the kids huddled together.

Nikki wondered how someone or something could sleep inside and outside at the same time? How did that make any sense? And why wouldn't it dream or wake up? Why would its face change in the daytime, and then again in the nighttime? The last part was the most confusing of all. How could something be dull and shining at the same time? Nikki hoped the others had more ideas than she did.

Peter Powerhats said, "My dad sometimes sleeps outside when he comes home really late. My mom tells me to stay away from him."

No one knew what to say to that, so no one said anything.

"We need an answer," Grunhilda said. "No answer is the same thing as a wrong answer."

Nikki shivered. She didn't want to find out what would happen if they couldn't figure out the riddle. Spencer was humming, which was a good sign. Samantha and Mike were whispering to each other. Axel and June were also deep in conversation. Nikki was nervous, so she just started talking. "I don't think the answer is a person," she said. She wasn't sure where she was going with this, but she felt better thinking out loud. "A person doesn't shine."

Spencer stopped humming. "True," he said. "And I've never heard of a person who doesn't dream."

"Good point," Samantha said. "Mike and I were thinking it might be a street light or something. There's a street light outside my house and it shines through the window, so it's sort of inside and outside at the same time."

"Is that your final answer?" Grunhilda asked.

"No!" all the kids said at once.

"Then hurry up!" the three birds said at the same time.

"Hmm," Spencer said, considering Samantha and Mike's idea. "That's really smart. But there are lots of things that could shine through windows, like car lights and porch lights."

Sue, who had been quiet the whole time, said, "Tell them what we're thinking, Sharkey."

Sharkey clacked her teeth together, and then said, "You all are thinking too small. There's a much bigger light that shines through windows. It shines through the night, and is dull during the day. It doesn't dream and it's always asleep because it's never really awake. And, of course, it changes its face depending on where it is in the sky."

"Very clever!" Spencer exclaimed. "I think you're right."

Nikki was even more confused. "In the sky? What do you—" All at once it clicked, and she figured out the answer that Sue, Sharkey, and Spencer had already come up with. "The moon!" she exclaimed.

Sharkey nodded excitedly as everyone congratulated her and Sue. Even Sue was smiling at all the attention. "That was *our* answer," she said. "It doesn't matter who said it, right?"

Seth said, "The Power Giver knows all things. You will be rewarded fairly." Sue smiled even bigger.

The Tri-Bird let out a shriek of anger. "That was the easiest riddle of all, you will not come up with the others so easily," Grunhilda said.

The second bird, Brunhilda, said, "The second riddle is this: What is as old as time itself, dancing while it eats, wearing a coat of many

126

colors, reds and oranges and yellows and blues, made by humans, made by nature, feeding billions of people all at once?"

Nikki blinked. Something about the riddle seemed so familiar to her. Although the other members of the Power Team were already discussing the riddle, she wasn't listening. She was staring at her hand, which was still covered in flames, like a torch, lighting the cave. Somewhere behind the light, she saw something move in the shadows. She blinked and looked harder, but whatever she'd seen was gone. She shook her head, refocusing on her hand. The flames were dancing. The hottest parts were blue, while the rest of it was red, orange and yellow. She'd made the fire, but she knew that nature could also make fire, like if a lightning strike hit something really dry, like brown grass. And, of course, at any given time there were fires all around the world, cooking food to feed billions of people.

"Fire," she whispered.

"What was that?" Spencer said. "What did you say, Nikki?" One by one each of the kids stopped talking to look at her.

Brunhilda said, "She said nothing. She knows nothing. Someone else must answer."

"But I *know* the answer," Nikki said.

The wrinkled old bird clawed toward her, its three beaks snapping at the air. "Do not speak, child!" they all said at once.

Seth stepped between the bird and Nikki. "Remember the rules," he said. "Any one of the kids can answer your riddles. He turned back to Nikki. "Go ahead."

Nikki stared into the six black eyes staring back at her. She wasn't scared of the Tri-Bird—not anymore. "Fire," she said.

The Tri-Bird screamed, as if it was in pain.

Spencer said, "Genius!"

The rest of the kids crowded around, patting her on the back and giving her high-fives. Even Sue said, "Good job, Nikki."

"Thank you," she said. Nikki was proud of herself, but she was still worried about the third riddle. It was probably the hardest of all.

"Go on then, Patsy," Seth said. "Last chance to stump us."

The third bird, Patsy, twisted around to face them. Somehow her beak seemed even longer and sharper than her two sisters. "The third riddle is this: I give you life and I kill you. I pull you down and lift you up. I am as hard as stone and soft as feathers. I am home to creatures beyond counting. I can be huge or small, wide or twisty. Who am I?"

The kids looked around at each other. No one spoke. Not even one word. Nikki got more and more nervous as the silence continued. The birds laughed occasionally, which only made Nikki more nervous. No one seemed to have an answer to the final riddle.

"Hello?" Patsy said. "Is anyone still here?" The bird took a clawed step closer to the kids, scraping the cave floor. It took all of Nikki's courage not to run away screaming.

"Give us a minute," Spencer said.

"We must have an answer!" all three birds shrieked at once.

"And you will," Spencer said. He turned to the rest of the group. "Anyone have a guess? We need something or Miss Cranky Bird isn't going to be too happy."

All the kids started talking at once, about anything and everything they could think of, but nothing made sense. Nothing fit all the clues in the riddle. The Tri-Bird stepped closer, its beaks open. "Time's up," Patsy said. "No answer is a wrong answer. Time to face the consequences."

Axel suddenly jumped out in front. "We have an answer," he said.

The Tri-Bird laughed. "Give us your false answer and let us judge."

Axel laughed back, not scared at all. "I'm feeling a little thirsty," he said.

Nikki frowned. *Thirsty? What was that supposed to mean? That wasn't even an answer.*

And yet Axel's words had a clear effect on the birds, who began shrieking and clawing at the dust. "No!" Patsy screamed. "You!" Brunhilda cawed. "Can't!" Grunhilda shrieked.

Nikki wasn't sure what was happening, until Axel spoke again. "I could really use some…"

"No! Don't say it!" the three birds screamed together, and Nikki realized the answer to the riddle.

"WATER!" the entire Power Team shouted together.

The Tri-Bird took off in a single motion, its six claws barely missing the kids as it swooped overhead, its six powerful wings flapping in perfect harmony. And where the bird once stood was a stone door, which swung open without a sound.

"THE POWER GIVER AWAITS!" a deep and scary voice boomed.

20

The Cave of Power

As it turns out, the deep and scary voice was just George Powerglasses shouting through a ginormous conch shell. With a wave, he beckoned the kids through the stone doorway.

"FOLLOW ME!" he said, still speaking through the shell.

The butterflies in Nikki's stomach seemed to be multiplying with each step. She was actually going to meet the Power Giver, the person who'd given her and the rest of the Power Team their powers. Beside her Spencer squeezed her hand and grinned—he was just as excited.

The tunnel George led them through started out rocky and rough, but soon became smooth and metallic. The metal was polished and shiny. "Is that..." Spencer said, running a hand along the even surface.

"Silver," George said. "Real silver."

"Wow," someone murmured behind Nikki. She thought it sounded like Chilly.

"Better than gold," Axel joked.

Nikki and the rest of the kids laughed. It felt good to laugh about the golden clouds now, like they were nothing more than a distant memory.

"Actually," George said, stopping for a moment. "The silver also has a strong and immediate impact on your powers."

Oh no, Nikki thought. *First gold and now silver?*

George laughed. "It's not what you think. Silver doesn't block your powers like gold does."

Nikki let out a sigh of relief. "Then what does silver do to them?" she asked.

Spencer answered for George. "Boosts them, right?" he said.

George nodded. "Bingo." He continued walking, leaving the Power Team to discuss the interesting turn of events.

"Why would the Power Giver want our powers strengthened when we meet him?" Freddy asked.

"Or her," Samantha said. "It could be a girl."

"Or a dog," Peter said. "I'm hoping for a dog. I like dogs." He barked three times and then pretended to wag his nonexistent tail. Nikki couldn't help but to chuckle a little. Peter was a bit...odd...sometimes, but he could also be pretty funny.

"Maybe the Power Giver uses the silver to strengthen his or her *own* powers," Spencer suggested.

Spencer's idea made sense. A lot of amazing things had been happening since they arrived on the Power Island. If the Power Giver's powers were being boosted by so much silver, that could explain everything.

"We should keep moving," Seth said, urging them along. George was already disappearing around a bend. "Sometimes the tunnel changes without warning."

Nikki wasn't sure what that meant, but she and the others hurried to catch up to George. The tunnel dipped, heading downhill, and for a while the walk was easy. But then it bottomed out and began to climb quite steeply. Soon Nikki's legs were aching and she was breathing hard. The rest of the Power Team was struggling too, except for Sue, who was breathing normally and smiling. "Pageant training," she said, when Nikki stared at her.

Finally, when Nikki wasn't sure whether she could take another step, the silver tunnel ended at a large, circular portal. It almost looked like an airlock on the space shuttles or space stations Nikki sometimes saw in the movies. George approached the portal and began doing all kinds of crazy things. First, he said, "Magnanimosquito," and then turned a weird futuristic-looking steering wheel. Next he spun a hand crank three times, tapped his toes together, and said "There's no place like Disney World. There's no place like Disney World." Last, but not least, he punched a code into an electronic keypad. Nikki read the code over his shoulder, just in case she ever needed it. *POW3R5*, it read. Three letters and three numbers, spelling out *POWERS*.

With a pop and a shudder, the portal opened, swinging inwards.

"AHHH!" a loud voice thundered. "MY GUESTS OF HONOR HAVE FINALLY ARRIVED!"

George waved them forward, ahead of him. "Ladies first," he said. "Age before beauty." Technically, they were all older than him by one second.

Inside the portal was an enormous, circular cavern. Like the tunnel, the curving walls were all completely smooth and sheathed in silver. *That'll boost our powers*, Nikki thought. *And the Power Giver's.* Even the floor beneath their feet was silver.

When all the kids were inside the silver dome, George and Seth stepped inside and the portal slammed shut. "Hey! What is this?" Sue complained. "Open the door."

"The door will only open once the final Power Rankings have been determined," George said. "Until then, make yourself at home."

Nikki looked around. The place was completely empty. She moved a few paces forward and her footsteps echoed ominously. "Where's the Power Giver?" she asked. Her hands were sweating and her heart was beating like an army of drummers.

The moment the question left her lips, a bright light flashed on from across the cavern, blinding her. She shielded her eyes with her hands. Nikki squinted, trying to peek between her fingers. A shadow the size of Tyrone when he was a Greek god crossed the room toward them. The shadow's long arms and hands seemed to stretch forward, trying to grab her. Dark tentacles flailed out in many directions, and black feathers sprouted from the creature's head. *Maybe Peter was right,* Nikki thought, *the Power Giver isn't a person, it's a creature. Not a dog, but a monster.*

Nikki backed up a step, crashing into whoever was behind her. She stepped on someone's foot and almost fell, but strong arms held her up on each side. *Axel and Tyrone,* Nikki realized when she twisted her head back and forth. They were squinting too, each using one hand to block the light.

Spencer, who always seemed to enjoy bright lights, stepped to the front. "We are the Power Team," Spencer said, "but you probably already know that, since you're the one that created us."

"YOU CREATED YOURSELF!" the powerful voice said, like the crashing of a wave. "I ONLY GAVE YOU WHAT YOU NEEDED TO FIND EACH OTHER."

"What would you have us do?" Spencer asked. She could tell her friend was getting a little nervous because he was dancing from foot to foot, almost as if he needed to pee.

"FIGHT!" the Power Giver roared.

Fight? Nikki thought. *But I thought we were supposed to be a team.*

"It's about time," Sue said. "I'm going to turn you all into peanut butter, and not the smooth kind."

"NO!" the Power Giver boomed. "NOT EACH OTHER."

"Then who?" Sue asked. Even squinty-eyed with her nose wrinkled in confusion, Nikki thought the pageant princess looked pretty.

"MEEEEE!" the Power Giver answered, the one-syllable word echoing through the silver cavern.

"Huh?" Spencer said as the Power Giver stepped into the light.

21

The Power Team vs. the Power Giver

Naomi had been following the rest of the Power Team for a while now. The truth was, she wasn't very good at riddles. She preferred real questions with real answers, like the tests she always aced at school. Riddles were too...abstract.

So she'd lurked in the shadows, staying just out of sight as the rest of the kids figured out the stupid Tri-Bird's stupid riddles. At one point Nikki Powergloves looked right at her, but Naomi was too quick. When George led them down the silver corridor, she'd followed from a distance. George was too focused forward to notice her, but Seth, who was at the very back, had turned around and winked at her. Luckily, he didn't tell anyone else that he saw her.

In the end, Naomi had barely managed to slip through the portal before it closed. No one saw her as she tiptoed around the edge, sticking to the shadows created by the Power Giver's bright light.

When the Power Giver challenged them to a fight, she shuddered, but no one saw her fear—they were too busy staring at the Power Giver.

Naomi was also staring, completely shocked by who had stepped into the light. The Power Giver wasn't a monster at all. He wasn't even scary. He was just a kid. Well, an older kid, a teenager, but a kid nonetheless, with acne and messy hair and glasses too big for his face. He was tall and skinny with dark skin that seemed to soak up the bright light shining on him. The weird tentacles they saw in the shadows were cast by a backpack with noodles strapped to it. Not the type of noodles in spaghetti and meatballs, but like the Styrofoam ones you played with in a swimming pool or at the beach. He was also wearing a feathered headdress. Like George had before, he held a conch shell, which is what he must've used to make his voice sound so loud and scary.

Naomi, forgetting that she was supposed to be hiding, almost said something like "You're just a stupid kid like us," but luckily Nikki's big-mouthed genius sidekick spoke first.

"*You're* the Power Giver?" he said.

"In the flesh," the Power Giver said.

"Oh," Spencer said, sounding disappointed.

Naomi understood how he felt. After all they'd been through to get here, she'd expected the Power Giver to be more…impressive. Not just some kid wearing a headdress and weird backpack, talking through a shell.

"But you're just a kid," Spencer said, echoing Naomi's thoughts. It was starting to scare her that she was thinking the same things as Spencer Quick.

"So are you," the Power Giver said. "All of you are 'just kids.'" The Power Giver used his fingers to make air-quotes. "At least that's what everyone tells you. Your parents, your teachers. But that's not true, is it? You've proven that. You've done incredible things with the powers I've given you. Some of you have used your powers for good, and others for, well, let's just call it not-so-good things." Naomi could've sworn the Power Giver glanced her way, his gaze cutting through the shadows.

"But only because you gave us powers," Britney said, her voice coming out as squeaky and nervous as a mouse. When the Power Giver looked at her, she went bright red.

"Your powers gave you confidence," the Power Giver said. "But you're the ones that had to learn to use them the right way."

Naomi cringed when she heard Sue's voice. It was like nails on a chalkboard to her. "He's right," Sue said. "I was already doing amazing things *before* I got my powers. I hadn't lost a single pageant since I was five years old."

Hearing Sue talk about winning pageants suddenly made Naomi realize something. Sue was exactly like her, except Naomi always won at school. She won every spelling bee, scored highest on every test, was the best Mathlete on the team. Sue wanted to win the Power Giver's ultimate prize every bit as much as Naomi did, which was exactly why they disliked each other so much.

To Naomi's surprise, the Power Giver was nodding in agreement with Sue. "She's right. You have all done incredible things during your short lifetimes, even before you received your powers. And you have the potential to do even more amazing things with the rest of your lives. The choice is yours and yours alone."

Naomi thought about his words. Did he mean winning? Or something else?

"But why did you bring us here?" Samantha asked. "Why are we competing in the Power Rankings?"

The Power Giver smiled. "I know I probably look like I'm still just a kid, but in less than ten minutes I'll turn eighteen years old. Technically, I'll be an adult. And an adult cannot be the Power Giver. It has to be a kid, pure and innocent and imaginative. In fact, when I become an adult, I'll no longer believe in superpowers. It's sad, I know, but true. I'll forget everything I've done the last eight years. All the good, all the mistakes, everything."

Spencer said, "Ohhh, I get it! Your birthday is the same day as the power kids!"

"The same second, actually," the Power Giver said. "I need one of you to replace me. The best, the strongest, the most talented, the wisest, the humblest. That's the ultimate prize."

Naomi's heart soared. He was talking about *her*. He had to be. She was *all* of those things. Well, maybe not the humblest, but everything else. She could do this. She could win and become the new Power Giver!

"How are you going to choose?" Axel asked. Naomi was wondering the same thing.

"Like I said before, you have to fight me. This is the last challenge and then the final Power Rankings will be tallied and whoever is at the top will be the winner. You have less than ten minutes to beat me."

"What if we don't beat you?" Tyrone asked.

The Power Giver paused, looking at each kid in turn. He even threw a look at Naomi in the shadows. *He knows I'm here*, she thought. Then he said, "If you don't defeat me, the powers will disappear forever. Even this island will vanish. All the magical creatures will be gone. The Weebles, the gnomes, the unicorns, the leprechauns. You'll all go back to your regular lives. Until you turn eighteen, you'll remember what you've lost."

A sad silence fell upon the cavern. The thought of losing all their powers seemed to suck all joy from the space.

"You have eight minutes left until you turn ten years old," the Power Giver warned. "You best get started."

All at once, there was a flurry of activity. Each power kid opened their powerchest, searching for the perfect powers to use. The sidekicks huddled up, strategizing on how to defeat the Power Giver. Hidden in the shadows, Naomi chose her own powerskirt, her favorite, the blue one that allowed her to change her powers as rapidly as Seth and George.

The Power Giver was already on the move, racing back toward the far side. Naomi watched as he raised an arm to the silver wall. First hundreds of platforms appeared. Hundreds upon hundreds of Weebles sat on them, cheering and taunting and bouncing up and down. Above them were the names of kids and rankings, from one all the way to twelve:

1. Axel Powerjackets
2. Nikki Powergloves
3. Sue Powerslippers
4. Naomi Powerskirts
5. Britney Powerearrings
6. Samantha Powerbelts
7. Jimmy Powerboots
8. Mike Powerscarves
9. Tyrone Powerbling
10. Tanya Powershirts
11. Freddy Powersocks
12. Peter Powerhats

Beneath the rankings was a clock, counting down. *7:45...7:44...7:43...* They were running out of time!

Naomi knew she had dropped from one to four because she didn't participate in the riddle challenge, but she also knew she could get back to #1. She'd done it before and she'd do it again.

She crept around the outside of the dome, planning to surprise the Power Giver with her laser winks, or maybe her flock of pigeons, but then he vanished. There was a blast of wind and something invisible knocked her over. When she climbed back to her feet, every other kid was lying flat on their backs, having been pushed over too. *He's invisible,* Naomi thought. *And really fast. And really strong.* "The silver is making him even more powerful," she whispered to herself. *And he has lots of powers...no...EVERY power.*

138

At the very moment that Naomi realized the full extent of the Power Giver's powers, Nikki Powergloves pushed to her feet and looked right at her. "He has everything," she said.

Naomi nodded. "He has *all* our powers."

"Jumpin' Pogo Sticks," Spencer said.

"We have to work as a team," Nikki said. "It's our only chance."

Naomi shook her head. She wasn't in this for them. She was in this to win. "Do what you want, but I'm going to defeat the Power Giver alone."

She felt the wind coming again, the invisible Power Giver racing toward her on feet as fast as lightning. Instantly, she changed her skirt to the pink one and then did a backflip. She went higher than ever before. The Power Giver rushed underneath her, missing completely. The rest of the power kids and their sidekicks did their best to get out of the way, too, but they were too slow. Once more, they were knocked flat on their backs.

Out of the corner of her eye, Naomi saw her name switch places with Sue's on the Power Rankings, moving from #4 to #3. She was already heading in the right direction!

But that's when the rest of the Power Team got smart. Let by Nikki Powergloves, they began to coordinate their powers. First Nikki told Peter to wear his purple jelly hat. When he scratched his head and asked "Why?" she shouted "Just do it!" So he did, his entire body turning to jelly a moment later.

The clock continued to count down. *6:23...*

The next time the Power Giver came around, Naomi executed a perfect back handspring to get out of the way. Nikki used her flying powers to hover in the air, and the invisible Power Giver ran smack into Jelly Peter. This time, however, Peter didn't fall over. The Power Giver ran right through him, leaving a hole that looked just like an seventeen-year-old boy. And the Power Giver was no longer invisible. Because he was covered in strawberry jelly, all the kids could see exactly where he was.

They attacked.

Samantha shot an enormous gob sticky gum from her fingers but the Power Giver used a mirror to deflect it back at her. She collapsed in a mess of gooey gunk, and her name dropped two spots in the rankings.

Freddy became a ninja turtle and tried to kick the Power Giver, but the teenager blocked it with a giant hand, throwing Freddy back. His turtle shell cracked off the wall and he dropped to last place in the rankings.

Mike was spinning faster than a tornado, but the Power Giver swung a long dinosaur tail out and tripped him.

Britney became a strange kind of monster, just a bunch of leaves swirling around in the outline of a person, but the Power Giver shot a powerful spray of water at her. Soon Britney was just a pile of wet leaves on the ground.

Jimmy attempted to use his ability to control objects with his mind to launch some of the Weebles at him, but the Power Giver created a dome of protection around him. The Weebles bounced off the dome and flew around the cavern, giggling uncontrollably.

Peter had changed from jelly back to his normal self, and started burping fireballs. They were way bigger than any fireballs he'd ever burped before, the size of cars. The Power Giver jumped back and shot a stream of ice, turning the fireballs into ice balls. He caught one in his giant hand and threw it at Peter. Peter tried to catch it, but the ice ball was so big it practically flattened him.

Tyrone was wearing a gold crown and dropping bombs onto the Power Giver's head. However, just before the bombs exploded on him, the Power Giver created a black hole and the bombs disappeared from this galaxy completely, gone forever into outer space.

Tanya transformed into a knight, complete with a gleaming sword and polished armor. She leapt forward, swinging her long blade at the Power Giver, moving incredibly fast. A shield appeared in the Power Giver's hand and he blocked her sword three times before using his other hand to shoot a dart into Tanya's leg. She immediately slumped to the ground and started snoring.

Even the sidekicks joined the action. Dexter sprayed Sticky Situation Glue while Spencer fired off his Alien Freeze Ray. In the chaos, Sharkey tried to bite the Power Giver's leg while Slobber and Weasel closed in from both sides. At the same time, Chilly Weathers pulled a rabbit out of a hat and sent it hopping into the fight.

Just before each of the sidekick's hit him, the Power Giver turned into a diamond, and everything just bounced off of him. The Sticky Situation glue stuck to him, but he was able to peel it away. A split-second later, he fired nets from his fingertips, trapping each of the sidekicks in a tight web of ropes.

Naomi stayed out of the way, using her gymnastics skills to dodge any projectiles that happened to fly her way. She watched the Power Rankings change rapidly as each kid tried, and failed, to defeat the Power Giver. He was simply too strong for them. But Naomi was still only #3, just ahead of Sue and just behind Nikki and Axel, and time was running out with only three minutes and six seconds left.

Sue was wearing her green lightning-bolt-shaped slippers. She raced toward the Power Giver, leaping a poisoned arrow and ducking a dozen red lasers he winked at her. When she reached him, she placed her hands on his head and shouted, "Mind muddler!"

The Power Giver staggered, almost fell, but then seemed to get control of himself. He shot a slime ball at Sue, hitting her in the eyes. "Can't see!" she said, running in circles until she got so dizzy she fell down.

Another competitor down, Naomi thought.

Next up was Axel, who was working together with his sidekick, June the Goon. June was the distraction, moving so fast it almost looked like she had powers. The Power Giver tried to whack her with his dinosaur tail, but she grabbed on, riding it like a bucking bronco. At the same time, she climbed his tail like a rope, pulling herself closer to the Power Giver, who began swatting at her with his giant hand. She dodged one slap and he smacked his own tail, bellowing in pain. Meanwhile, when the Power Giver was distracted, Axel attacked from the other side with a stampede of cows. He rode the one in the front, charging with reckless abandon. The Power Giver turned, surprised, and June managed to leap on his head, covering his eyes with her hands. "Gotcha!" she exclaimed.

Naomi thought for sure that the Axel/June team was going to win, but then the Power Giver started to transform. His eyes turned to headlights, his hands and feet to wheels, and soon he was a red Ferrari. With the squeal of tires, the Power Giver raced away, leaving June to smell the burning rubber and exhaust. The cows tried to turn but ran into each other. Axel flew off his cow, and the moment he hit the ground the stampede disappeared.

There were only two minutes left on the clock!

Axel dropped to #3 in the Power Rankings. Naomi hadn't really done anything, and yet she was back at #2. Nikki Powergloves was #1. *Not for long*, Naomi thought.

She prepared to jump into the fight, carefully selecting her black skirt. She'd only ever used it once before. It hadn't worked the first time, but she knew this time would be different.

Nikki Powergloves, however, beat her to it, diving from the air at the red Ferrari. A bolt of ice shot from her fingertips, freezing all four tires at once. The Power Giver slid to a stop and transformed back into himself. Then he started to grow. And grow. And GROW. He grew until he was almost as tall as the entire cavern, ducking to avoid hitting the silver roof. He was using Tyrone's power to become a Greek god. He swung a car-sized fist at Nikki, but she managed to fly out of the way, firing streams of ice. The ice hit the Power Giver, and for a moment he appeared to be frozen. The Weebles cheered.

But then the ice began to crack. Icicles and chunks of ice rained down from above, and Naomi had to run and dive to avoid getting hit. The Power Giver swung another punch at Nikki, but this time he changed direction at the last second, grabbing her with fingers the size of tree trunks. "MWAHAHAHA!" he laughed.

Naomi knew this might be her only chance. She concentrated on the bright lights shining from the walls. As the Power Giver laughed, his chuckle shaking the entire cavern, sparks began to fly. Bolts of electricity crackled and then shot outwards. The Power Giver stopped laughing as he was hit from all sides by the high-voltage attack. His giant body went rigid and he started to shake. Naomi knew shocking the Power Giver wouldn't be enough. She needed to do something unexpected, something completely and utterly insane.

She switched to her purple skirt.

There was only one minute left.

And then she mixed up the world.

22

And the winner shall be…

Nikki's whole body felt as if it had been shoved in a blender, then microwaved, then rolled down a flight of stairs, and then squeezed by a trash compactor.

Yeah, she was feeling sore. She wasn't even sure what had happened. All she knew was that the Power Giver had grabbed her, squeezed her, and let her go. She'd tumbled to the floor, her head spinning, her bones aching.

From there, things got even weirder.

Up became down and down up. Silver became gold and then back to silver. The air turned to water and suddenly she was swimming. She held her breath until her lungs ached. Finally, the water vanished and she fell, rolling around the silver dome, which seemed to be moving like a hamster's wheel.

As Nikki rolled, she saw the other kids rolling, too, along with the Weebles. Spencer was shouting strange words, like "Tootsie!" and "Sloppy Joe!" The Power Giver was flopping around like a fish out of water, his giant Greek god body slamming against the walls, which began to crack and bend from the impact.

In the very center of the rolling dome was Naomi, floating in midair, her arms stretched to each side. Her face was full of glee, her eyes as big as silver dollars. The Power Rankings rolled around and around, and each time they showed Naomi Powerskirts as #1, and Nikki as #2. There were only thirty seconds left on the countdown.

Nikki knew it was over, knew she had lost, knew that the power kid she wanted least to win, had won. Naomi would become the Power Giver and the rest of them would get their powers taken away by her.

But as the walls crumbled around them, Nikki thought it might be even worse than that. Naomi was so out of control that she might actually destroy *everything*. The Power Island, the world, the entire universe. Who knew what she was capable of doing with the power of her purple skirt.

Nikki's eyes met Naomi's and something changed in her old enemy's expression. She looked almost...sad. "This doesn't feel the way I thought it would," Naomi said.

Nikki's teeth chattered as she tried to speak. "W-winning only m-means something if y-you d-do it the r-right way," she said.

Naomi cocked her head to the side, looking more innocent than Nikki had ever seen her. She nodded slowly. "I think I finally understand. I have something to tell you all. Something to tell the Power Giver."

The Power Giver managed to say, "SPEAK NOW." The clock read twenty seconds.

"I cheated," Naomi said. "I've always cheated. My parents would've been disappointed if I wasn't the best in school. So I cheated. I stole tests, looked off of other kids' papers, and wrote answers on my hand. I knew most of the answers, but still, I cheated. And today, I cheated again. I didn't know any of the riddles. I let you all answer them for me, and then I snuck in behind you. I don't deserve to be here. I deserve to be last."

Nikki was shocked. It was the last thing she expected Naomi to say with only ten seconds remaining before her birthday. Before all their birthdays.

"Wow," Naomi said, "telling the truth felt really good. I feel so much…better. Now it's your turn Nikki. On the count of three, get ready."

Somehow, some way, Nikki knew exactly what Naomi meant.

"One!" Naomi said.

While still rolling, Nikki opened her powerchest and switched her ice glove for the brown one.

"Two!" Naomi said.

Nikki tensed her muscles, preparing for the most important moment of her life.

"Three!" Naomi said.

Everything stopped rolling and the dome settled back into position with an earth-shaking *BOOM!* Up was up again. Down was down. Gravity worked the way it was meant to. The Power Giver groaned and tried to roll over, but Nikki was already changing, already pouncing. She had fur and a lithe sinewy body and sharp claws and a mouth that could—

"ROAR!" she bellowed, leaping on top of the Greek god. Nikki the Lion was bigger and stronger than she'd ever been before, thanks to the power of the silver dome.

The Power Giver was so scared he started shrinking, getting smaller and smaller until he was just a seventeen-year-old teenager about to have a birthday.

"Uncle!" he said. "You win. Nikki, you win." The clock stopped on one second and time seemed to stand still. And then it changed to *0:00*.

Nikki leapt off of the Power Giver and let out a final roar of victory. As she gazed at the rankings on the wall, she watched as her name passed Naomi's for the final time and the Weebles cheered. The rest of the Power Team crowded around her, patting her lion's fur and congratulating her.

146

The Power Giver looked at his watch. "It's time," he said. "I have a one minute grace period before I'll forget everything about this place."

Lioness Nikki changed back into Nikki Powergloves. "What's going to happen?" she asked.

The Power Giver shrugged, his dark eyes sparkling. "I guess we'll find out," he said. "The Power Giver before me didn't know either."

"But how will I know what to do?" Nikki asked. All her excitement at having won the Power Rankings was already beginning to fade as the truth of the situation began to settle in. *She* was the Power Giver now. And she didn't even know exactly what that meant.

"You'll know," the Power Giver said with a wink. "Trust me, you'll know. The most important thing is that you be true to yourself, and always try to do what's right. The rest will take care of itself."

With his last word spoken, a white mist rose up around the Power Giver's feet. "Ah!" he said. "That tickles! Happy birthday, Nikki. And happy birthday to all the rest of the power kids!" As Nikki and her friends looked on in awe, the white mist began to spin around the Power Giver like a tornado, pulling the feathered headdress off his head and wrenching the Styrofoam noodles from his backpack.

"HAPPY BIRTHDAY, POWER GIVER!" Nikki and her friends shouted. The Power Giver smiled and spun and then vanished in a shower of gold and silver sparks. Above them, hundreds of kids appeared like stars in the night sky, smiling and looking down. They almost looked like ghosts; but no, they were their ancestors—the power kids who had come before them. Some wore hats, some belts, some shirts, some gold bling, some earrings, some socks, some scarves, some jackets, some boots, some skirts, some slippers, some undies, some glasses—and yes, some wore gloves. Powergloves.

Eventually, they vanished, too, just like the Power Giver.

The Power Team continued to gaze at the ceiling, mesmerized by what they'd just witnessed. But not Nikki. She knew she had a job to do, and to do it she'd have to look forward and not back. Starting with Naomi, who she'd just spotted trying to sneak out of the cavern.

"Stop," Nikki said, and Naomi did. When she turned around, Nikki expected Naomi to be angry, defiant, full of her usual pride and toughness.

But instead she found a broken girl. "I'm sorry," Naomi said. "I'm sorry for everything."

"You did a lot of bad stuff," Nikki said. "You hurt a lot of people."

"I know."

"You cheated in the Power Rankings."

Naomi nodded. Her bottom lip quivered, but she didn't cry. Even in defeat, she was a really strong girl.

Which was exactly why Nikki knew she needed her. "I want you on my Power Team," Nikki said.

Naomi's eyebrows shot up. "What? No. I *cheated*, remember? All I wanted was to win, no matter what the cost. I didn't care about being the Power Giver, or helping people, or anything but myself. You don't want someone like that on your team." This was the Naomi that Nikki remembered. Fiery, argumentative, bold. She was still in there. If only Nikki could convince her to use all her good qualities for *good*...

"I forgive you," Nikki said. "In the end, you did the right thing. You told the truth. That's what matters. That's who you are."

"But I—thank you," Naomi said. "But the others..."

"Will forgive you too," Nikki said. "Remember Tanya? Remember Jimmy? Remember Tyrone? They're part of our team now, too. And so are you, if you want to be."

"I..." Naomi paused, her face tensed in serious thought. "I..." Suddenly her expression lit up in a huge smile. "Yes! Yes, I'll be on the Power Team. For real this time."

Nikki gave her a hug and Naomi stiffened at first, but then relaxed, hugging her back. "Thank you for everything," Naomi said. "You really are the true Power Giver. I'll do my best with the powers I have."

Nikki laughed. "But maybe only use your purple skirt in emergency situations."

Naomi managed to laugh too. "Deal," she said.

Nikki realized the rest of the kids had been watching and listening to most of their conversation. Freddy and Mike were scowling. So were Dexter and Chilly. "Guys," she said. "Naomi and I have come to an agreement. I really don't want to argue about this. Please accept her as part of the—"

"Of course!" Mike said, his frown changing to a smile in an instant. "We were just messing with you." Freddy, Dexter and Chilly smiled too. They crowded around Naomi and welcomed her to the team. So did the rest of the power kids and their sidekicks.

Well, except for Jimmy, who was hanging back from the others with his new sidekick, Slobber. Nikki was about to go to them and see what was going on, but Naomi beat her to it. "I'm so sorry, Jimmy," Naomi said. "I treated you really badly on the Power Outlaws. I should've been nicer. I should've listened to your ideas." She turned to Slobber, who took a step back, as if scared. "And I'm sorry about treating you like a servant. You should've been my partner. I couldn't see past winning, and I'm sorry I was so mean to you."

Jimmy and Slobber looked shocked, their tongues hanging out of their mouths as they tried to speak. "I, uh, oh, okay. Thanks. Cool," Jimmy said. Then, almost as an afterthought, he said, "Slobber was your sidekick. I can find another."

Slobber said, "Thanksh, Naomi. Thanksh."

Naomi shook her head. "No," she said. "I was the wrong power kid for Slobber. You're the right one. He should still be your sidekick."

Jimmy and Slobber's eyes lit up. They had already become friends. They gave each other a high-five. "Aweshome!" Slobber said.

"And we'll help you find a new sidekick," Jimmy promised. "We'll hold the second ever Sidekick Auditions."

"Thanks!" Naomi said. She looked genuinely excited at Jimmy's idea.

Nikki smiled. Her team was already shaping up to be pretty good. *No, not just pretty good*, she thought. *The best.*

Someone else approached her, with long, sun-drenched blond hair and a perfect smile. "You deserved to win, Nikki," Sue said, flashing straight rows of perfectly white teeth.

"You don't mean that," Nikki said. She used to find it hard to see through Sue's lies, but not anymore.

A flash of anger crossed Sue's face. "You're right. I don't mean it! It should've been me. Anyone with one good eye can see that *I'm* the best choice for Power Giver. I'm the prettiest, aren't I? Have you seen my hair? Have you seen my *smile*? Judges in fourteen counties agreed that I should win. They would've laughed you off the stage."

Nikki sighed. Someday Sue might be able to change, might be able to realize that it wasn't all about looks. It was about being honest, kind, and real. Glitz, glamor, makeup, and rehearsed answers to questions might be what it took to win in Sue's world, but not on the Power Team. But Sue wasn't going to realize that today. When she was ready, she would understand. And when she did, Nikki would be ready to welcome Sue back with open arms. Everyone deserved a second chance. Or even a third, or fourth.

"Sorry, Sue, but I have to let you go," Nikki said.

"What!?" Sue shrieked. "Let *me* go? I don't take orders from you. You're not *my* Power Giver."

But Nikki had already made up her mind. She could feel the power flowing through her. It was a power she didn't take lightly. It was the power to *choose*. She could choose which kids got powers, and which didn't.

Nikki squeezed her hand into a fist, feeling warmth in her fingers. And when she opened her hand, there was a single tiny powerchest. "When you're truly ready to change, come find me," Nikki said, "and you can have this back."

"What? Is this some trick? That's not my powerchest—that's *your* powerchest." Sue was checking her pockets, trying to find what Nikki had already taken from her. "No!" she screamed when she realized she'd lost her chest full of slippers. "No! I'm Sue Powerslippers! I can't go back! I can't go back to the endless shopping for pageant outfits and new hairstyles and memorizing stupid answers to stupid questions and learning how to walk and turn. Please, Nikki. *I can't!*"

"Goodbye, Sue," Nikki said, and Sue was gone in the blink of an eye. After all, even at the very end, Sue was acting. *One day*, Nikki thought. *One day she'll be back as a friend.* Even though Nikki knew she'd done the right thing, it still hurt to do it. Her heart ached just a little.

Luckily, she was surrounded by friends to support her. And they did. They talked and laughed and all agreed that she'd done the right thing and that Sue would eventually come around, just like Naomi had.

And when they were done talking and laughing, Spencer yelled, "PARTY!" Weebles, who seemed very good at knowing when and where a party was about to break out, appeared on the platforms around them. Music began playing as they jumped down. Everyone started dancing, as more and more friends appeared. There were the familiar Weebles, Bo Diddy (who was already challenging some of the kids to a dance competition), Roy (who was once more dressed up like a bride in wedding gown), and the Great Weeble (who was spinning on his head and shouting "Yeehaw!" over and over again). The gnomes popped from holes in the ground that Nikki didn't even know were there. They removed their hats and bowed low to each kid, wishing them a happy birthday. Then they started shaking their butts and dancing like everyone else. Unicorns pranced gracefully through the crowd. Even the elf whose gold Nikki had almost stolen during the Great Adventure was there, standing in a corner and guarding a large pot overflowing with shiny coins. Cranky the Crab made a brief appearance, but left soon after, muttering about "Noise, so much noise!"

Seth was wearing four pairs of underwear on the outside: one in normal position, one on an arm, one on a leg, and one on his head like a crown. He'd even let Spencer borrow a pair so he could have a tight white crown too.

George was riding his purple-winged Pegasus and shooting rainbows across the cavern. When he caught Nikki looking at him, he lowered his glasses and winked at her, as if he always knew she would win. She smiled. He would be a great ally to have, as smart as he was powerful.

When the kids were too tired to dance anymore, they took the tunnel back outside and sat along the cliff, staring into the rolling field of lava. Nikki craned her head back to look at the stars, which were sparkling like diamonds in the sky.

"Let's talk powers," Nikki said. "What are you going to use your powers for?"

Nikki was surprised when Britney was the first to speak. "Well, I had this idea…" she started, and then she told the Power Team what she wanted to do.

As Nikki listened to each kid explain what they wanted to do with their powers, she couldn't stop smiling. Everything was going to be just fine. She had THE BEST Power Team she could ever ask for.

And when they finished, she knew it was time to say goodbye, at least for a while. It was their birthday, and they should be spending it with their families. "Go home," she said. "All of you. We'll start work a week from now, in the Power City. See you all there!"

23

A new world
One year later

Nikki Powergloves, the Power Giver, would turn eleven years old later that day, along with the rest of her Power Team. George Powerglasses and Seth Powerundies would too, although technically they'd turn eleven one second after the rest of the power kids.

Although she was excited about the birthday party they had planned, Nikki tried to concentrate on the letters she'd received from each of her friends. She was so proud of them all. In only a year, they'd done so much for the world. With the Power Team looking out for everyone, they were creating a new world one power at a time.

The idea Britney Powerearrings had come up with a year ago while sitting on the cliff on the Power Island had turned into a reality. Using her pink flower earrings she'd made the world even more beautiful, creating gorgeous flower beds in neighborhoods that used to be all concrete and asphalt. She called her little project (which was really a *big* project) Flower Power. She'd even found a sidekick they nicknamed

Greenie, who had an especially green thumb. Greenie helped Britney maintain the hundreds of flower beds, watering, pulling weeds, and pruning them. The people in each community would actually cheer whenever Britney and Greenie showed up. Of course, Britney would turn bright red each time. She still wasn't used to all the attention, which Nikki thought was a good thing.

Samantha Powerbelts had taken to the oceans, wearing her blue "snorkel" belt to work with damaged coral reefs and marine life, repairing the reefs and rescuing injured sea creatures. As it turns out, being able to breath underwater was a very good talent to have for that kind of work. She had the full support of a major marine conservation agency. Dexter was also behind her a hundred percent. Although he wasn't much of a swimmer himself, he assisted in the planning of her missions, learning everything there was to know about sea life.

Freddy Powersocks had focused on nature, too, but on land, rather than in the water. He was known worldwide as the Animal Whisperer, using his white, polka-dotted socks to talk to injured animals. Knowing exactly what was hurting them and how they were feeling was very helpful in treating their injuries and caring for them. And Chilly Weather's love and compassion for animals made her the perfect sidekick to help him find more animals in need. So far, they'd helped save thousands of animals.

Mike Powerscarves had been using his favorite power—provided by his green "ice cream cone" scarf—to provide food for the hungry. He supplied healthy food to soup kitchens across the country, as well as to shelters and refugee camps worldwide. He hadn't found a sidekick yet—he was too busy for that—but Nikki knew he would eventually.

Coming from a military background, Axel Powerjackets and June the Goon had decided to work on world peace. In the beginning, it had seemed like an impossible challenge, but they were beginning to have success. Using his impressive array of powers, and June's formidable abilities, they'd managed to stop several conflicts before they started. When half your army was stuck with darts that made you sleep for ten hours, it made it hard to fight the enemy. True peace would be a long and difficult process, but at least things were headed in the right direction.

Jimmy Powerboots was in a million places at once…literally. The first thing he'd done after explaining his idea, was to clone himself. And then his clones made clones. And more clones. Until there was an army of Jimmys. Then he'd discovered he could clone Slobber, too, so he did. Soon every Jimmy-clone had a Slobber-clone. In the past, that might've been a dangerous thing, but not anymore. Now Jimmy and Slobber were helping the world as part of a disaster relief team that would go to areas that had major earthquakes, hurricanes, tornadoes, tsunamis, or other terrible disasters. The Jimmys would use their ability to move objects with their minds, while the Slobbers would use their natural God-given strength to help clean things up, repair houses, and get the people back to normal life as quickly as possible.

Peter Powerhats? Well, he was still Peter Powerhats. His Las Vegas show continued to be the most popular in town, making people laugh three times a day with his antics. Although some of the other power kids thought Peter could do more with his powers, sometimes the power of laughter was as important as anything else.

Naomi Powerskirts had been true to her word, and was a committed member of the team. She'd learned that she could use her ability to travel on a beam of sunlight to take other people with her. So many people were separated from their loved ones by great distances, and Naomi was able to bring them together for a short time. As promised, Jimmy and Slobber had held a Sidekick Audition and found her the perfect sidekick, a kid named Moses Magoo, who was very organized and great at filling out forms. There was a lot of paperwork when it came to bringing people across country borders, and Moses made sure that everything they did was strictly legal and authorized. Each of Naomi's customers were very satisfied.

Tyrone Powerbling had come up with an idea with the help of his sidekick, Weasel. Weasel was a reformed girl. She felt bad about all the things she'd stolen in the past, and now wanted to help catch thieves and return stolen items to their rightful owners. Tyrone's powers came in handy when it came to catching thieves. So far they'd apprehended sixty-four thieves and returned dozens of stolen items to their owners, including sixteen purses, twenty-six wallets, three million dollars stolen from eight different banks, and even a priceless Ming vase heisted from a museum in Europe. A spokesperson for the FBI was quoted as saying that the duo were "the most valuable crime-stoppers we've ever seen."

Tanya Powershirts had a lot of really scary powers, and she was putting them to good use in Africa and Asia. She'd singlehandedly managed to decrease the amount of poaching that occurred by half. Hunters who were illegally hunting elephants for their tusks, rhinos for their horns, tigers, zebras and bears for their skins/furs, or gorillas so they could sell their babies, came to fear Tanya, who might show up in the lush jungles of Thailand or the hot plains of Africa at any time, usually with an army of skeletons behind her. Or she might be a tarantula or a bog monster, chasing off the animal killers before they could harm any of the defenseless creatures. Nature conservationists loved Tanya. They even voted for her to win one of their most prestigious awards!

George Powerglasses and Seth Powerundies were Nikki's advisors, helping her track and oversee all the good work that her Power Team was doing. They had become her good friends at the same time. Spencer Quick, boy genius, was still her sidekick and best friend, helping her decide where to use her own powers, just like in the beginning in Cragglyville, a time that felt like a million years ago.

When Nikki finished reviewing all the reports from her Power Team, she leaned back and sighed. Life was good. Together, they were making each day better than the last. They were normal kids part of the time, going to school, doing homework, making friends and playing, and superheroes the rest of the time. Balancing everything was hard, but they were doing it one day at a time. Yeah, they had amazing powers that helped them along the way, but what amazed Nikki the most was all of the *other* kids who'd joined in their efforts. In the last few months a movement had started in a small town in South Dakota called Buffalo. The kids there had been inspired by the Power Team, and had decided to get involved, starting a campaign to do one random act of kindness every single day. Sometimes it was something simple, like letting someone go in front of them in line at the grocery store, and other times it was bigger things, like helping an elderly person pull weeds or searching for someone's lost dog or cat.

In any case, the movement had caught the attention of the local news, and then the national news, and soon kids all over the world had joined in, thousands upon thousands of kids trying to make the world just a little bit better. *Every kid HAS powers*, Nikki realized. They didn't need gloves or hats or anything else to use their powers. They had their brains and their muscles and their *hearts*. No one could take those away from them, and they could choose to use all their talents for good or evil. Nikki hoped they'd chose good, following the example her Power Team was trying to set for the world.

Finally, it came time for the big birthday party, and Nikki was overwhelmed with excitement as each of her friends began showing up. Last to arrive was Spencer, who said he had a big surprise for her.

Beside him was Sue, who looked just a little bit scared. She was still beautiful, but there was something different about her. Spencer said, "It's okay. Just tell her."

Sue shook her head and took a step back.

Spencer said, "She's ready."

Nikki smiled. Even without Sue saying a single word, Nikki knew this wasn't another one of her acts. For maybe the first time in her life, the real Sue was here. "I know," Nikki said. "Welcome." Nikki pulled out the powerchest she'd been keeping safe for the last year, the one full of amazing slippers. She held out her hand to Sue.

Sue's eyes grew as big as blue planets as she stepped forward. But when she reached for her old powerchest, it disappeared. She gasped and her arm dropped to her side. The old Sue would've been angry, would've said mean things. But this was a different Sue, the real Sue. "It's okay," she said. "I've joined the Random Acts campaign, and I think I'm pretty good at it. Even if I'm not on the Power Team, I'm still with all of you in spirit."

Nikki couldn't stop smiling. Her team was now complete. Sue didn't know it, but she was the last member. She was always meant to be on the team. "Check your pockets," Nikki said.

And when Sue did, her breath caught and her eyes got even bigger. She pulled her hand out and opened it. A single golden powerchest rested in her palm.

"Welcome back," Nikki said.

THE END, BUT NOT THE REAL END
THE STORY CONTINUES IN YOUR IMAGINATION

###

Are you a teacher or librarian interested in having an author speak in person or via Skype at your school or library? If so, please contact the author at davidestesbooks@gmail.com. The author also welcomes requests from interested parents and their children.

Power Team Card

Hidden Identity: Nikki Powergloves
Birth Name: Nikki Nickerson
Age: 9
Height: 4 feet, 2 inches
Weight: 67 pounds
Sidekick: Spencer Quick, certified genius
Known Allies: the entire Power Team and their sidekicks
Source of Power: Gloves

Powers

Glove Color	Glove Picture	Power
White	Snowflake	Create ice
Red	Flame	Create fire
Light blue	Bird	Fly
Black & yellow	Lightning Bolt	Control the weather
Green	Leaf	Super-grow plants
Purple	Muscly arm	Super-strength
Orange	Shoes	Super-speed
Gray	No picture	Invisibility
Brown	Paw print	Transform into an animal
Pink	Tarot card	See the future
Gold	Clock	Freeze or slow down time
Peach	Two identical stick figures	Transform into someone else

Power Team Card

Hidden Identity: Samantha Powerbelts
Birth Name: Samantha Jane McKinley
Age: 9
Height: 4 feet, 6 inches
Weight: 77 pounds
Sidekick: Dexter Chan, excellent booby trapper
Known Allies: the entire Power Team and their sidekicks
Source of Power: Belts

Powers

Belt Color	Belt Picture	Power
Brown	Dancing teddy bear	Make objects come to life
Peach	Six-armed girl	Grow extra arms/legs
Multi-colored	Paintbrush	Change objects' color
Silver	Shield	Dome of protection
Gold	Key	Open any door/lock
Bright red	Smile	Make people laugh
White	Gum	Shoot sticky stuff
Blue	Snorkel	Breathe underwater
Orange	Rope	Shoot ropes from hands
Clear	Diamonds	Turn rocks to jewels
Green	Walking trees	Make trees come alive
Yellow	Spider	Climb walls like a spider

Power Team Card

Hidden Identity: Freddy Powersocks
Birth Name: Frederick Nixon
Age: 9
Height: 4 feet, 5 inches
Weight: 95 pounds
Sidekick: Chilly Weathers, amateur magician
Known Allies: the entire Power Team and their sidekicks
Source of Power: Socks

Powers

Sock Color	Sock Picture	Power
White with black polka dots	Dog barking at a boy	Ability to speak to animals
Gray	Astronaut	Anti-gravity
Camouflage	Chameleon	Camouflage himself
Gold	Wristwatch	Change rate of time
Black	Nunchucks	Ninja skills
Peach	Girl slapping a boy	Distance slap
Pink	Brain	Read people's thoughts
Brown	Shovel	Dig huge tunnels
Black & Yellow	Bumblebee	Turn into a bumblebee
Purple	Microphone	Impersonate voices
Green	Turtle shell	Grow a shell
Fuzzy brown	Monkey	Control a horde of monkeys

Power Team Card

Hidden Identity: Mike Powerscarves
Birth Name: Michael Jones
Age: 9
Height: 4 feet, 2 inches
Weight: 67 pounds
Sidekick: None
Known Allies: the entire Power Team and their sidekicks
Source of Power: Scarves

Powers

Scarf Color	Scarf Picture	Power
Black	Car tire	Turn body to rubber
Blue/Gold striped	Tall pole	Leap high in the air
Gray	Hammer	Ability to build anything
Green	Ice cream cone	Create food
Brown striped	Tornado	Spin tornado-fast
Red & Yellow polka dots	10 stick figures	Break into 10 mini-Mikes
Black & white	Magnifying glass	Disappear sideways
All colors checkered	Plus sign	Boost other kids' powers
White	Steering wheel	Drive any vehicle
Brown & black checkered	Minus sign	Decrease other kids' powers
Orange	Hovercraft	Ride a hovercraft
Green & red polka dots	Dinosaur tail	Grow dinosaur tail

Power Team Card

Hidden Identity: Britney Powerearrings
Birth Name: Britney Mosely
Age: 9
Height: 4 feet, 2 inches
Weight: 63 pounds
Sidekick: Jen Green (nicknamed "Greenie")
Known Allies: the entire Power Team and their sidekicks
Source of Power: Earrings

Powers

Earring Color	Earring Shape	Power
Silver	Large hoops	Super discs
Red	Hearts	Love potion
Blue	Butterflies	Change into butterfly
Clear	Diamonds	Become as hard as diamonds
Gold	Small hoops	Mini discs
Black	Long dangly	Pixie sticks
Green	Leaves	Leaf monster
Pink	Flowers	Soft flower bed
Brown	Feathers	Pointy feather attack
White	Angel wings	Grow angel wings
Silver with turquoise stone	Square with inlaid gem	Create big stone blocks
Red ruby	Gemstones	Red laser beams

Power Team Card

Hidden Identity: Axel Powerjackets
Birth Name: Axel Grant
Age: 9
Height: 4 feet, 8 inches
Weight: 75 pounds
Sidekick: Juniper (June the Goon) David, hero in training
Known Allies: the entire Power Team and their sidekicks
Source of Power: Jackets

Powers

Jacket Color	Jacket Picture	Power
Blue denim	Feathered darts	Dart gun
Black leather	Ghost	Ghost attack
Beige cloth	Cow	Cow stampede
Blue windbreaker	Eagle	Sprout wings
Heavy gray wool	Slinky	Slinky movement
Blue & red flannel	Ape wearing a crown	Turn into King Kong
Red nylon	Rocket	Turn into a missile
Green pullover	Elf	Elf mischief
White sweatshirt	Ski poles	Super skier
Dark orange fleece	Orange fruit	Become a giant orange
Brown tattered zip-up	Boot	Big boot
Yellow stylish	Ferrari	Yellow Ferrari driver

Power Team Card

Hidden Identity: Jimmy Powerboots (previously known as Jimmy- Boy Wonder)

Birth Name: Timothy Jonathan Sykes (nicknamed Jimmy)

Age: 9

Height: 4 feet, 1 inch

Weight: 65 pounds

Sidekick: Dante James, nicknamed "Slobber"

Known Allies: the entire Power Team and their sidekicks

Source of Power: Boots

Powers

Boot Color	Boot Picture	Power
Black	Cracked ground	Powerstomp
Purple	One leg on each side of a wall	Walk through walls
Orange	Floating bananas	Move objects with mind
Red	Boots with flame	Rocket boots
White	5 identical stick figures	Clone himself
Yellow	Half-boy here, half-boy there	Teleport
Blue	Wall of water	Control water
Brown	Big ear	Super senses
Green	Computer	Computer hacking
Red/blue/yellow	Wires	Skills with electronics
Gray	Yellow pages	Find anyone in the world
Gold & black checkered	Clock	Speed up time

Power Team Card

Hidden Identity: Peter Powerhats
Birth Name: Peter Hurley
Age: 9
Height: 4 feet, 10 inch
Weight: 100 pounds
Sidekick: unknown
Known Allies: the entire Power Team and their sidekicks
Source of Power: Hats

Powers

Hat Color	Hat Picture	Power
Bright gold	Powerchest	Find lost powerchests
Neon green	Strong man	Grow big and strong
Black	Cannonball	Turn into cannonball
Gray	Stones	Makes stones form
Red	Bull horns	Transform into a raging bull
Peach	Big hand	Grow big hands
Blue	Big wheels	Drive a monster truck
Orange	Mouth and fire	Burp fireballs
Green	Fingers holding nose	Stinky farts
Purple	Strawberry jelly	Turn body to jelly
Brown	Porcupine	Cover body in prickly spines
Clear	Teardrops	Make people cry

Power Team Card

Hidden Identity: Tyrone Powerbling
Birth Name: Tyrone Mitchell
Age: 9
Height: 5 feet, 2 inches
Weight: 110 pounds
Sidekick: Weasel (real name unknown)
Known Allies: the entire Power Team and their sidekicks
Source of Power: Bling (jewelry)

Powers

Bling Color	Type of Bling	Power
Gold	Watch	Turn into a Cyclops
Gold	Stud earrings	Become a Greek god
Gold	Chain bracelets	Make things bigger
Gold	Ring	Make things smaller
Gold	Thin necklace	Super-punch!
Gold	Crown	Drop bombs
Gold	Walking stick	Shoot torpedoes
Gold	Belt buckle	Ride a wild mustang
Gold	Chain necklace	Become Paul Bunyan
Gold	Pocket watch	Create black holes
Gold	Sunglasses	Drive a race car
Gold	Thick bracelet	Drive an Egyptian chariot

Power Team Card

Hidden Identity: Sue Powerslippers
Birth Name: Susan Hopper
Age: 9
Height: 4 feet, 0 inches
Weight: 55 pounds
Sidekick: Shakti Shahara, nicknamed "Sharkey"
Known Allies: the entire Power Team and their sidekicks
Source of Power: Slippers

Powers

Slipper Color	Slipper Design	Power
Green	Lightning bolt shaped	Mind muddler
Pink	Ballet slippers	Light on her feet
Silver	Metal	Robo Sue
White	Feathery	Grow bird wings
Blue & yellow	Shooting stars	Falling star attack
Yellow	Ducks	Quack attack
Brown	Moccasins	Shoot poisoned arrows
Green	Crocodile skin	Turn into a crocodile
Black	Snakeskin	Turn people to stone with her eyes
Blue	Fluffy	Turn into a mermaid
Purple	Poofy	Create big bubbles
Gray and white striped	Knitted	Become a Greek goddess

Power Team Card

Hidden Identity: Tanya Powershirts
Birth Name: Tanya O'Rourke
Age: 9
Height: 4 feet, 6 inches
Weight: 70 pounds
Sidekick: unknown
Known Allies: the entire Power Team and their sidekicks
Source of Power: Shirts

Powers

Shirt Color	Shirt Picture	Power
Gray	Shark's teeth	Become a shark
Black	Skeleton	Skeleton army
White	Guy hanging onto a light pole	Control the wind
Red	Spider	Become a tarantula
Orange	Balloon	Take off like a hot air balloon
Ble	Car	Transform into a car
White & black striped	Mummy	Create mummies
Brown	Weird creature	Become a bog monster
Green	Green splat	Shoot slime balls
Silver	Knight	Suit of armor
Black	Closed eye	Cause temporary blindness
Charcoal	Big mouth	Super-shout!

Power Team Card

Hidden Identity: Naomi Powerskirts
Birth Name: Naomi Lee
Age: 9
Height: 4 feet, 0 inches
Weight: 55 pounds
Sidekick: Moses Magoo
Known Allies: the entire Power Team and their sidekicks
Source of Power: Skirts

Powers

Skirt Color	Skirt Picture	Power
Yellow	Sun	Travel on light beams
Green	Ogre	Turn into an ugly monster
Blue	Three skirts	Change powers fast
Black	Light bulb	Control electricity
Brown	Mud	Create gobs of mud
Pink	Gymnast	Gymnastics skills
Purple	Mirror	Mix up the world
Gray	Foot on water	Walk on anything
Orange	Closed eye	Laser winks
Pink & black striped	Skateboard	Skateboarding skills
Black with green polka dots	Plant with arms	Grow fighting plants
Turquoise	Pigeon	Attack pigeons

Power Team Card

Hidden Identity: George Powerglasses
Birth Name: George Kennedy
Age: 9
Height: 4 feet, 3 ¾ inches
Weight: 77 pounds
Sidekick: None
Known Allies: the entire Power Team and their sidekicks
Source of Power: Google Glasses

Powers

Lens Color	Lens Symbol	Power
Green	Venus fly trap	Turn people into plants
Purple	Pegasus	Pegasus appears
Red	Ring of fire	Human torch with laser eyes
Blue	Dolphin	Grow fins and flipper
Black	Panther	Transform into panther
Brown	Globe	GPS locator
White	Black outline of person	See invisibility
Reflective silver	Oval mirror	Deflect attacks
Yellow	Sunburst	Flash bang!
Rainbow	Rainbow	Create rainbows
Neon pink	A hand	"Borrow" powers
Iron gray	Wall	Big metal wall
Clear	Raindrops	Giant raindrops

Power Team Card

Hidden Identity: Seth Powerundies (Calls himself UnderMan!)
Birth Name: Seth Joyner
Age: 9
Height: Average
Weight: Skinny
Sidekick: None
Known Allies: the entire Power Team and their sidekicks
Source of Power: Undies

Powers

Undies Color	Undies Symbol	Power
Tighty Whities	Blimp	Undies turn into a giant blimp
Tighty Whities	Slingshot	Shoots himself out of a giant slingshot
Tighty Whities	Bug	Bug zapper
Tighty Whities	Ball	Hide in a protective ball of undies
Tighty Whities	Trampoline	Undies stretch into a trampoline
Tighty Whities	Shirt and trousers	Create undie clothing
Tighty Whities	Snowshoes	Undie snowshoes
Tighty Whities	Springs	Pogo-shoes
Tighty Whities	Swiss cheese	Holes in his body
Tighty Whities	Pipes	Human pipeline
Tighty Whities	??? (invent your own fun undie powers!)	
Tighty Whities	??? (invent your own fun undie powers!)	
Tighty Whities	??? (invent your own fun undie powers!)	
Tighty Whities	??? (invent your own fun undie powers!)	

Acknowledgements

This book, like all the others in the series, are for kids all around the world to enjoy. You are my reason for writing about Nikki and her adventures!

A Greek-goddess-sized thank you to my wife, Adele, for sticking with me through the ups and downs and always being my voice of reason.

A silver-powered thank you and a big-handed fist bump to my own Power Team of kid beta readers and their 3rd grade teacher, Mrs. Clanton, as well as her exceptionally clever granddaughter, Katee. Words cannot express how awesome all of you are. Thank you to her class of 2015: Braden Routier, Sydnee Thompson, Sheridan Reedy, Rhett Connors, Clancy Adolph, Claire Verhulst, Slate Page, and Riggs Rotenberger! These kids are so clever and imaginative that I have to give them full credit for coming up with the idea for at least three parts of this book as follows: 1) the giant onion slicing itself and making all the kids cry; 2) Opposite Day; and 3) that silver enhances the kids' powers. YOU came up with these ideas, thank you for letting me borrow them for this book!

Lastly, thank you to my cover artist and friend, Tony Wilson at Winkipop Designs, whose own imagination gave this series the perfect look and feel!

Discover other books by David Estes available through the author's official website: http://davidestesbooks.blogspot.com or through select online retailers including Amazon.

<u>Children's Books by David Estes</u>

The Nikki Powergloves Adventures:
Nikki Powergloves- A Hero is Born
Nikki Powergloves and the Power Council
Nikki Powergloves and the Power Trappers
Nikki Powergloves and the Great Adventure
Nikki Powergloves vs. the Power Outlaws
Nikki Powergloves and the Power Giver

<u>Young-Adult Books by David Estes</u>

The Dwellers Saga:
Book One—The Moon Dwellers
Book Two—The Star Dwellers
Book Three—The Sun Dwellers
Book Four—The Earth Dwellers

The Country Saga (A Dwellers Saga sister series):
Book One—Fire Country
Book Two—Ice Country
Book Three—Water & Storm Country
Book Four—The Earth Dwellers

Salem's Revenge:
Book One—Brew
Book Two—Boil
Book Three—Burn

The Slip Trilogy:
Book One—Slip
Book Two—Grip
Book Three—Flip

I Am Touch

The Evolution Trilogy:
Book One—Angel Evolution
Book Two—Demon Evolution
Book Three—Archangel Evolution

Connect with David Estes Online

Facebook:
http://www.facebook.com/pages/David-Estes/130852990343920

Author's blog:
http://davidestesbooks.blogspot.com

Smashwords:
http://www.smashwords.com/profile/view/davidestes100

Goodreads author page: http://www.goodreads.com/davidestesbooks

Twitter:
https://twitter.com/#!/davidestesbooks

About the Author

After growing up in Pittsburgh, Pennsylvania, David Estes moved to Sydney, Australia, where he met his wife, Adele. Now they travel the world writing and reading and taking photographs.

Made in the USA
Middletown, DE
14 January 2016